ONDINE'S CURSE

ONDINE'S CURSE

a novel by

STEVEN MANNERS

Porcepic Books
an imprint of

Beach Holme Publishing
Vancouver

This book is published by Beach Holme Publishing, 226–2040 West 12th Avenue, Vancouver, B.C. V6J 2G2. This is a Porcepic Book.

The publisher gratefully acknowledges the financial support of the Canada Council for the Arts and of the British Columbia Arts Council. The publisher also acknowledges the financial assistance received from the Government of Canada through the Book Publishing Industry Development Program (BPIDP) for its publishing activities.

The Canada Council | Le Conseil des Arts
for the Arts | du Canada

BRITISH
COLUMBIA
ARTS COUNCIL
Supported by the Province of British Columbia

Editor: Michael Carroll
Production and Design: Jen Hamilton
Cover Art: *Die Suende (Sin)* by Franz von Stuck, 34⁷/⁸" x 21¹/¹⁶", oil. Collection of the Frye Art Museum, Seattle, Washington. Used with permission.
Interior Photograph: *Cross on Mount Royal*, National Archives of Canada, PA-202810
Author Photograph: Jack Berry

Printed and bound in Canada by Tri-Graphic

Canadian Cataloguing in Publication Data

Manners, Steven, 1957-
  Ondine's curse

  "A Porcepic book."
  ISBN 0-88878-409-0

  I. Title.
PS8576.A562O52 2000   C813'.54   C00-910661-8
PR9199.3.M3492O52 2000

For those who believed

ACKNOWLEDGEMENTS

For information on Shawnadithit and the Beothuk language, I am indebted to *Shawnaditti: The Last of the Beothucks* by Keith Winter (North Vancouver: J. J. Douglas, 1975).

"Good Night, Irene," words and music by Huddie Ledbetter and John Lomax copyright © 1936 by Ludlow Music Inc. Copyright renewed 1964 by Ludlow Music Inc., New York, New York.

"Ich bin von Kopf bis Fuss auf Liebe eingestellt." Friedrich Hollaender copyright © 1930 by Ufaton Verlagsgesellschaft mbH.

I am grateful for the kind support of the Ontario Arts Council.

I

The principal disease of man is an irresistible curiosity filled with
anxiety that he may not know something.
—Blaise Pascal

Montreal is the greatest underground city in the world.
—Statement at the Opening of the Métro Extension

The rats are agitated tonight. The radio is playing as they swarm over the river embankment, turning and turning over the wet flagstones, flicking wet tails. Then there is the noise, the scream of tight falsettos climbing into the ultrasonic like claws along your spine. You can't hear it over the radio, an old one with solid-state transistors and imitation-leather carrying case that the rats are now chewing to shit with their scissor teeth. Sewer rats, Rattus norvegicus. *Trained in a laboratory to work those buttons. (Don't touch that dial.)*

Then the station slips, and the night air is filled with radiomancy, the superstations and satellite miscues that seep out old pop tunes and call-in shows, Edward R. Murrow and blitz-bomb effects, voices and sounds like lost souls in a maelstrom of atmospheric disturbance until one of them—that one there, the big brown fucker with the red eyes and bald head—gets inside and nips the wires.

Whoever undertakes to write a biography binds himself to lying, to concealment... Truth is not accessible.

—Dr. Sigmund Freud

Names come to mind immediately who are agents provocateurs; well-paid, well-established in the media and who are, I think, social saboteurs.

—René Lévesque

ONE

December 1989. The air was crisp that day, early winter. On the mountain, the sky over Montreal was glass—sharp, crystal. Sounds carried in the rarified air. Ondine could hear the traffic downtown whispering like a rumour. A man's voice was shouting a mile off, angry words that would thaw only in the spring. In the far distance, the harbour and an alarm bell ringing.

She had spent the morning at the university library, sifting through the stacks of books, the dust as exotic to her as archaeology. She had expected to be there only an hour or so, but her research had taken longer. She was looking for aboriginal accounts, first-person records of life at the turn of the century—the nineteenth century, Ondine's area of interest. The documents were dog-eared, over-thumbed, used up. She needed something original. She didn't keep track of the hours. It was hard to predict how long things would take. She was three years behind on her thesis.

Ondine could have worked longer, but she had arranged to meet someone—a man—in the afternoon. She had a sandwich at the cafeteria, then caught a bus over the mountain to the French university.

There was snow on the ground. The view over the city was beautiful, almost painful. The light soft at this hour, red-tinged aura. But that is how they always describe it: the prodrome.

The afternoon air was colder, hard on the lungs. As she looked at the view, a word came to mind: *breathtaking*. It took her breath. Maybe that had something to do with it, the oxygen/carbon-dioxide balance. She would be told that as she would be told many things.

"We've set up a canopy apparatus to test your breathing, your sensitivity to CO_2."

"Will that help, Doctor?"

"I should think it will make you feel a good deal worse. But it will give us enormous insight."

On the mountain that day she might have imagined the oxygen getting thinner. There was a tendency to hallucinate, to see things. The beauties and horrors of the world. Holy men, gnostics, visionaries climbed mountains. Was there something on the horizon, out at sea? Were they there as witnesses, martyrs? Did they know what was yet to come? Did Ondine?

No. It was the naive period, terrible in its optimism. Ondine did not yet believe in animism, the evil that inhabited buildings, intersections, moments in time.

"Had you consumed any street drugs that day? Marijuana, cocaine?"

"No."

"No other drugs?"

"I had a coffee. Two. I smoked a cigarette."

"And then what?"

"I went inside."

She was unprepared when the attack came. There was no warning. Or perhaps there was—a sign, omen, electromagnetics on the mountain realigning like a topographic map—but she had noticed nothing. Something about being outside in the cold, then crossing over, the building stuffy, overwrought. Question of atmospherics.

"Can you describe your cognitive content?"

No. Nothing. She was there to meet a friend. Her mind was

blank. Did that absence of thought, of feeling, create a vacuum? Was it an invitation? Yes. Something had to move in to fill it.

Enter the Terror, fear like she had never known. She panicked. She ran. Across the parking lot to a fringe of trees. Through the underbrush to a dirt track, then beyond to a chainlink fence that kept the mountain at bay. She ducked through a hole in the fence, panting now, her breath biting great holes in the air, the thin air. At the top of the hill she stumbled, fell. She was in a cemetery: frozen plaques, dendrite trees, death everywhere and that damned red sky. The wind cold out of the northeast, rale of a plastic bag caught in a tree like a suffocated lung. Numb as she followed the asphalt path. Too tired to run, but her mind still fleeing. Toward the road girdling the mountain, the long climb up the slope in the dark.

Ondine didn't know how much time passed, impossible to predict. She climbed until she couldn't climb anymore. She huddled against the cold under the lights of the giant cross that loomed over the city. She knelt in the snow, chilled with cold sweat, lungs scratchy as sandpaper.

Wet snow falling. She shivered uncontrollably as if gripped by seizure. No, no cognitive content. Her thoughts were pure as the driven. Mind only reading static as if the signals were jammed. She was afraid she had gone mad.

Then the clarity. No more interference; she understood now. She had failed to see the omens, had ignored the symptoms. But here was a sign right before her—a monumental cross burning with lights that were visible for miles. She saw it now for what it was: God's bombsight.

TWO

Robert Strasser completes the sound check—one two three—and adjusts the video camera on the tripod. He drapes the lavalier microphone over the back of the empty chair, waits for the talent. It is his thousandth interview, give or take. At his apartment he keeps the recorded voices on shelves in an area he calls the tape morgue.

He used to play the tapes for women he'd invite over for coffee, every life like milk barely skimmed, a touch of celebrity in an otherwise uncelebrated evening. But the tapes have deteriorated with time and he has started to throw them away. Something about unexamined lives not worth keeping.

Only it is no good. They come back. In the night he can hear them: synchronous, everybody talking at once, out of context, as alien as television leaks into deep space. When the TV's on, he can hear the voices intruding like conversation on a talk show on some other channel. Their comments are urgent, their opinions endless.

They interrupt when he tries to sleep. When he makes love, they mutter obscenities.

Dr. Werther Acheson arrives, imposing, shock of white hair, ancient as hell. His bio says he was born in Germany, 1901. As old as the century. "Are you feeling all right, Doctor?"

Acheson irritably waves away the question; he's heard it before. He has heard everything before.

"If you're ready, we can begin. You understand—"

"Yes, yes."

Strasser ignores the impatience in his tone, explains anyway. "This is for our television program on CFIB every Wednesday night. *Notable Lives*. Have you watched it?"

"I do not study television."

"You don't study it."

Acheson settles himself in the chair. "Why do you not?"

Strasser clips the microphone onto the doctor's lapel. Acheson has all the signs of advanced age: neck heavily wrinkled, skin mottled with liver spots, unshakable ideas. Years of lab work have destroyed his hands. His nails are yellow and misshapen, his fingers have white acid scars as if so much time could erode identity.

"When you got that gold medal at that meeting…"

"The World Psychiatric Congress, yes."

"It generated a lot of local interest."

"Did it indeed? So you have decided that you wish to know more about my work?"

"Your life," Strasser says.

"That is my work."

"Our listeners aren't up on their science, so we thought we'd focus on how you got started. Tell me how all of this—" the gesture vague enough to encompass the books, the stacks of paper on the desk "—began."

"Where do you wish to start?"

Strasser isn't entirely sure there's a story here, but he will find one. "Wherever you like."

"You must begin with an idea," Acheson objects. "What is it you wish from me?"

"I thought that would come out as we got into it."

"That does not seem a sensible plan."

"Nevertheless," Strasser says patiently, "all we can do is try and see what happens. I plan to interview some of your colleagues at the Institute. They can fill me in on some of the details about your work here, the day-to-day research. But I need the human side. People are always curious about how someone gets started. No one knows very much about your early days, the formative years. You came here from Germany, didn't you? Maybe we can start with that. There must be some colourful anecdotes from your past."

"Colourful, yes."

"Something visual," Strasser adds, already thinking ahead to the edit, "something that will let us cut away to some stock footage."

Dr. Acheson nods, as if he had been expecting something like this. "History begins with our century."

"Not yet," Strasser says. "I haven't turned on the camera yet."

"This is not for the camera. It is a sound check, yes?"

"Right."

Acheson begins again. "Your audience—they know only what they see on television. You give them history, pictures. So many pictures: the wars, bread lines, astronauts, movie stars. What of the other things—ideas, the dreams we pursue so madly? What about the other centuries? We do not know. There is no video, so we know nothing of those times. They were not so photogenic, I think."

"That's fine," Strasser says. "Camera's rolling."

THREE

When he was young, Strasser would listen for the rats in the alley outside his bedroom window. They would come up from the sewers—filthy, primitive, vile—like the reptiles in a Japanese monster flick. The rats scrabbled over the pavement, emitted high-pitched, unearthly sounds, tipped over garbage cans. They were big bastards, maybe two or three pounds each. They ate anything to survive: garbage, kitchen scrapings, their own shit, each other. Strasser's father set out poison in the alley. They ate the warfarin, the box, the warning label of a rat with a red cross through it. They didn't care. They came back the next night for more.

Strasser invented the game out of necessity. When he heard the rats at night, he would slide open his bedroom window and, waiting for just the right moment, flick on a flashlight. The rat, momentarily blinded, would freeze in the cone of light. It was childishly simple to pick them off with a BB gun. A head shot, a glancing blow to a rubbery haunch. The BBs wouldn't kill the rats, not at first. But with a bellyful of warfarin, the bleeding wouldn't stop. In the morning he would find the thin blood trails leading back to the sewer grate.

Strasser always had good aim, a good sense of distance and tracking, talents that would prove useful as a cameraman.

FOUR

R ecord...
Begin in the *Aufbruch* years, that frenzied manic time after
the war. The Great War, as they called it in America, the one in black
and white. Germany was destroyed, the middle class had peddled
its illusions, the country was broke.

It was a time of upheaval. The rules had changed: there were
no rules. For young Werther Acheson, the revolution would be
in medicine. His father, a chemist at Farbenfabriken Bayer in Elberfeld,
had worked with the great Heinrich Dreser, a rotund, balding
gentleman with a walrus moustache, head of the Pharmacological
Laboratory at Bayer. Acheson Sr. had worked on the laboratory's
greatest discoveries—Euspirin, later known as aspirin; and heroin,
the heroic drug, one of Dreser's pet *Morphinderivates*. Acheson Sr.
always spoke with reverence of the great man, even after their

famous quarrel when Acheson published his report of heroin's toxicity in *Münchener Medizinische Wochenschrift*.

The article was open on Dreser's desk when Acheson Sr. was summoned to his office. "Perhaps, Herr Doctor, you can explain."

"I have studied the substance. Heroin does not make the old people stronger," Acheson Sr. said. "They lie in their beds. They are in pain. They count the minutes until their next injection. What use is a drug that people can only hunger for?"

"Indeed, Herr Acheson, what use is a drug that creates no demand?"

The professor's comment remained with Acheson Sr. long after he had resigned and moved the family to Darmstadt, where he found employment at the E. Merck factory. His project was the barbiturate Veronal, which Merck would later license to Bayer. It was during that period that young Werther met with his accident.

An anecdote. It was summer and the family had gone on vacation to the Black Forest near Freiburg, the hometown of Herr Freud. The sun was hot, there were many other families picnicking by the river. Papa had shed his normally dour mood for something else. He seemed unusually affectionate toward Werther's mother that day, teasing her with comments that the boy did not understand. Werther became agitated, acted out, caused a fuss. Sensing his distress, Mama told her husband to take the boy for a walk by the river.

Werther punished his father with silence.

"You do not understand, boy," Papa said, which caused Werther to flush with anger. "One day everything will be revealed."

They paused by a dead tree, needle branches a cephalograph on the water. In the decaying trunk Papa spied a beehive and pointed it out to Werther. "You see the structure, the polygons, the perfect symmetry?" Papa asked, slipping easily into the tone he used in his lectures at the laboratory. "The great Kekulé dreamed of a snake biting its tail and conceived of the benzene ring."

"I know, Papa. You have told me."

"Or did he dream of benzene and awoke with the image of a snake?" Acheson Sr. asked darkly. Werther did not understood; he had not steeped himself in morphine derivatives, barbiturates, the genealogy of amphetamines. "The body is the Ur-Market, Werther, the manufactory of desire. That is the serpent in the garden of science."

For Werther such talk of desire was a wool suit on a June day; it chafed and irritated him. As Papa turned away, Werther dropped a large stone on the beehive, crushing the elaborate polygons. Then an eruption: a swarm of bees emerged from the tree and attacked them. "What have you done?" Papa cried as the bees stung him on the face and neck. He grabbed his son's hand and rushed to the river's edge. They hesitated only a moment—the bees in that instant sensing something—before plunging into the dark waters. The shock of cold struck Werther full in the chest. He felt a spasm of pain as he emerged from the water, coughing, eyes streaming. Papa was struggling toward the shore, gasping, clutching his chest, seized by apoplexy.

A woman helped Werther out of the water as a picnicker ministered to his father. Werther saw the waxy pallor, his father's blue lips as the strangers tried to revive him, and rubbed his chest where his own pain had been. Was his reaction beta-sympathetic or sympathetic, a form of magic, wish fulfillment? *Tödestrieb*, Thanatos. Had not Herr Freud himself said that all sons desire the death of the father?

Change tapes.

"You're talking about something that happened ninety years ago," Strasser says. "I'm surprised you can remember so many details."

"It is a story." Acheson shrugs. "I was told of it many years later. The events themselves I cannot recall. The symptoms erased everything."

Werther did not remember the bee that stung him on the head. It was a minor incident, easily forgotten. Later the nerve specialists would cite a bee sting as the cause of a lesion on Werther's brain.

The affected area was small, almost undetectable, but enough to produce epileptic symptoms. There were still flashbacks from that time, memories that were fin de siècle, gone impressionist hazy with the fugues, the outsized dreams, a sensation of small things grown large, the aura that Acheson would come to recognize as an impending attack.

A year later, when Acheson was nine, his déjà vu experiences began: compelling dysmnesic symptoms as electrical discharges coursed through his mind, disturbing his thoughts, upsetting his emotions. He saw images that he imagined he had seen before. Or was this only another circularity, ellipsis or epilepsis, as in all stories, fables, *volsungasaga*? Time multiplied upon itself, each moment refracted sixfold like a polygon, an insect's eye. A smell— the scent of a lover, odour of spilled milk from his mother's breast, a breath of autumn—could unearth a moment long buried. The brain relinquished nothing. A strange power, being unable to forget. Unlike history, which forgets everything.

FIVE

The lobby of the Institute is rotunda: circular, mahogany panelling, vaulted ceiling. The architecture, the structure, is a remnant, something left over from the turn of the century. Tilt to film the top of the dome and the sensation is one of falling up into the dome below you, into a layer of air undisturbed for a hundred years.

Strasser lugs his gear out to the truck but returns to book appointments with Acheson's colleagues. There is little he can use from the morning's interview, and he's going to need tape. He can use the bit about Bayer, insert photographs of the Black Forest, go for nostalgia, something in sepia. But bees, childhood guilt over his father's death? What is he to do with that?

Perhaps tomorrow's interview will be better. He's scheduled for an hour a day with Acheson. Strasser will keep each encounter brief to cut the rambling to a minimum. Acheson has lived his life too long to see its story structure. That is Strasser's job. He'll dig out the highlights, work it together into some sort of narrative. It won't matter that Acheson doesn't see the turning points, the plot points. The audience will see them. They won't need much from the formative years, except for hints of greatness. They can skip the errors, small failures, moments of indecision, months and years frittered away.

The amount that Acheson can recall from the early days is remarkable. But Strasser knows he'll have to keep him on track. Bring him into the present. Acheson will, of course, resist the pull. The old man has already shown a tendency to shuffleplay through time, idle too long in the eddies of memory, forget where he is headed because the drift is always downriver—to the unloved present, to here and now, to death.

The receptionist buzzes Dr. Baum, but the research director isn't in his office. "He may be down the hall," a nurse offers, "the *filmtherapie* group."

Inside the auditorium it is December 1941 in Casablanca—what time is it in Montreal? An onscreen Rick is entertaining Ilsa in his apartment. She's got a gun, but her hand is trembling. "You're here for the best part," the nurse says as she ushers him down the aisle. Strasser peers in the dark, tries to spot Dr. Baum, but it's no good. There are only filmgoing types, festival groupies, film aficionados watching silently as Rick and Ilsa kiss.

Fade out, fade in, and Rick is smoking a cigarette by the window. *"And then...?"*

"Best part?"

"The fade-out," the nurse explains. "It's diagnostic."

Audience faces a soft strobe in the blink of black and white. She is there by the exit sign, a young woman with black hair to the shoulders, face beautiful in a blank sort of way as she watches the screen. Her expression is too dark for video, but Strasser records her features in one-quarter profile, memorizing the distant half-moon of her face. He's still studying the woman as he whispers, "Diagnostic?" to the nurse.

"Ilsa's gone to Rick's apartment for the letters of transit," the nurse explains. "Yeah, right. He refuses. She pulls a gun but can't shoot him. They kiss. Fade to black. A second later she's on the couch, and he's standing by the window. So what happened in the fade-out?"

Strasser shrugs. "Nothing. Time passed."

"You ask the paranoid personality types, they'll tell you Rick and Ilsa were doing the dirty."

"Maybe they're right."

"They usually are." The nurse nods toward a group of heads along the far wall. "Paranoids," she whispers as she gives him the layout of the place. "Obsessive-compulsives in the centre—I mean the exact centre—of the room. Social phobes at the back, bulimics near the bathroom."

"What about by the door?" Strasser asks, but is disappointed to see that the woman has slipped out.

"Our famous sign," the nurse says with faint disapproval. Strasser sees that someone has changed the sign to read NO EXIT. "One of the analysands in the existential group." Wearily she adds, "They can be a handful."

"Is everyone in here a patient?"

"Sometimes the staff come in when they're on break."

"Who is that?" Strasser asks, nodding toward an older man sitting square in the aisle, rocking his body back and forth as he watches the screen.

"That's Dr. Kotzwara," the nurse says. "This is his show."

"Do you think he'd agree to an interview?"

"Not when he's in Group. Look for him tomorrow morning on the métro."

SIX

It was a year after broadcast school—a hick college full of farm-town hopefuls, FM wannabes trained in herd behaviour, hog calling—that Strasser got his big break. He was working at the time for a low-watt radio station, one of the media farm teams that sent its signal out to the highway like an SOS. The wave upon wave of broadcast signals were the fabric, the station manager liked to tell Strasser, the warp and weft holding the country together. Only late at night, with the hiss of a blizzard hitting the windshield like static, Strasser wondered if the waves were an ocean, skimming the surface over something dark below.

"Overnight low of minus four with a probability of precipita-tion…" Strasser cranked the wipers, but through the windshield it was just TV. Images ghostly and unreal caught in the headlights were a screen for your worst imaginings: jacklit deer, crazed hitchhikers, convicts bogarting at the side of the road. Strasser was navigating by instruments, staring into the swirl of snow and listening to the border station WWII-FM—What's-In-It-For-Me from the station that loves you best—when he saw the car ahead suddenly slew to the side of the road. The taillights winked out, gone. In the high beams he saw tire tracks leading nowhere. At the bottom of a steep gully, the car was lying on its roof, wheels spinning against a blacktop sky. He heard a woman crying in the dark.

He clambered down and tried to open the door, but the lock was frozen or had jammed on impact. "Is everyone all right?" Inside the wreck, an old woman was hanging, suspended by her seat belt. Strasser smashed the passenger window, unfastened the belt, and tried to ease the woman into a sitting position.

She cried out in pain. "My leg is caught. I think it's broken. Do you have a phone?"

"What happened?"

"I was taking poor Rudy to the vet. He was upset. I was trying to get him settled. Then something happened. Is Rudy all right?"

In the well of the passenger seat Strasser saw a collapsed cage. The cat was not moving. "You should keep talking," Strasser told her, "so you don't go into shock."

"I'm cold," the old woman complained. "My leg hurts."

"I know. Try to keep talking."

"What do you want me to say?"

"Anything. Tell me a bit about yourself."

They talked for an hour, Strasser half lying in the car, snow drifting in and out of the open window like consciousness until the tape ran out and cold killed the batteries. Strasser pocketed his tape recorder and climbed up to his car. He called the paramedics, but by the time they arrived the woman had died of internal injuries, blood loss. Strasser's report—the woman's dying words, a few pickup quotes from the paramedics—made the six o'clock news. It would later get him a Golden Microphone Award for Spot News Coverage and a TV job in the bigs.

SEVEN

Focus, focus…
They venture down the steps in ones and twos, no one together, everyone maintaining distance. They squint at the arc lamp Strasser has set up by the turnstile, blinded, shuffling uncertainly toward the light. The beam cuts through the dust in the air, searching out head shots like phrenology.

They are mostly young, mostly women. Blondes, brunettes, unremarkable at first glance. A cross section of people Strasser would never think twice about if he were to see them on the street, in cafés and burger joints, on college campuses. But there is something odd here. Their eyes betray them. They scan the ticket booth, pan along the tile walls, left and right and back again. Their eyes never stop moving. They pause at the shadows, staring into the unlit places as if their minds were heat-seeking, infrared. They gather around the videolight like moths.

"Who are you?" a voice booms out in the subway acoustics. Pan over to a large man in a Freudian goatee, two-piece safari suit, and Aussie bush hat, earphones dangling. "I'm Emil Kotzwara. I hope to God you're Strasser."

"I called your office," Strasser confirms. "They told me to meet you here."

"I got the message." Kotzwara fumbles with a cassette player hooked to his belt, rap lyrics leaking out. "One of my patients," he explains, "uses rap to express his manic symptoms. 'I can foretell all hist'ry/But men still diss me/*Ma blonde* she lets me juice her/And then she calls me Luc'fer/my gun is cocked/And I wanna rock…' And so on." He yawns. "Grandiosity, sexual aggression, some psychosis, of course." He switches off the tape. "What did you want to see me about?"

"An interview. I'm putting together a piece on Dr. Acheson. A Notable Life."

"Indeed."

"I was hoping you could lend some perspective to Dr. Acheson's work."

Kotzwara nods curtly. "Just checking. The métro attracts a certain element, a real diagnostic grab bag down here. One can't be too careful."

Kotzwara's group is aboard, so Strasser strikes the set. The doors hiss closed and the métro descends along the tunnel. Kotzwara poses at the front of the car as the subway careens through the darkness, but it's a video dead zone. Strasser can't hold the frame, and the ambient noise is all over the dial. "That's enough for now, Doctor," Strasser shouts over the noise. "Where are we headed?"

"Downtown. The shopping centre."

"Stores aren't open yet."

"That's my Friday group—compulsive shoppers," says Kotzwara, allowing himself a brief, unamused laugh. "This lot is panic disorder. We're here for our immersion therapy."

Seems the brain is wired like a home alarm, Kotzwara explains, stimulus triggering the locus ceruleus, a rather curious blue spot located deep in the brain. "Damnedest thing," he says. "Stimulate the LC and the subject gets anxious, avoidant, ready to fly at a moment's notice. The brain's distant early warning. They end up like this," he says, gesturing discreetly to the patients at the rear of the car, "always keeping an eye out, expecting trouble. What we refer to in the trade as 'limbic hyperarousal.' Hypervigilance. What you media boys might call an unreasonable fear response."

"What are they afraid of?"

"The usual. Going crazy, having a heart attack, dying in the street. What people nowadays always fear—insanity, mortality, anonymity."

"What sets them off?"

"Life. A lot of them were anxious as children. Maybe they suffered some trauma, maybe street drugs made them freak. It doesn't really matter. Even if we can't find the trigger, the gun still goes off."

Whatever the cause, the effect is overwhelming. Strasser can't imagine walking down the street or along a hall and suddenly being seized by panic: sweating, heart racing, can't breathe. As if the air had become a vacuum and collapsed the sky. Doom descending. The attacks lasted only a few minutes, but in that space everything would change. Reactions distorted, buildings shape-shifted, the street altered to a Munchian freeze-frame. As if Terror itself had raised its head to street level.

"The mind, you understand, is a nasty bit of software," Kotzwara says. "The poor beggars develop tremendous anxiety waiting for the proverbial axe to fall. That damned Damoclean sword. You get on a bus and you feel panic. You go out on the street and you feel panic. It's not too long before you start to associate certain places, a time of day, a set of circumstances with the terrible fear you're feeling. So you avoid those places."

"Are you saying they become conditioned?"

"Wouldn't you?"

Each panic attack like a bomb destroying a section of city. A downtown store: devastated. A campus green: razed. The Vieux

Port: obliterated. Each attack levelling more of the city until the only safe place is home.

"But you're saying this panicky feeling isn't a reaction to something?" Strasser asks. "Nothing real?"

"It's real to them. It may start as something real enough, post-traumatic and all that. Perhaps a car accident, a random act of violence, warfare. In Dr. Acheson's day they called it 'soldier's heart.' The young men in the trenches couldn't take the shelling. Some developed extreme anxiety reactions—palpitations, difficulty breathing, that sort of thing—as if they were having a heart attack. Even after they'd been demobbed, the lads would lie about in their beds panting like dogs, waiting for the next bomb to go off."

The medics would see them after a shelling, white faces like moons reflected in the puddles at the bottom of the trenches, lying in a universe of shit. They were not wounded, but the explosions never stopped in their minds. In the early part of the war they were moved to a hospital behind the lines, but they were lost, the terror never went away. Everyone had a theory to explain the symptoms: the men were weaklings, inferior specimens, their constitutions were degenerate.

Acheson was the junior member of the team and listened with deference to his colleagues' theories. But he was dissatisfied and offered his own ideas during rounds. "Is it not true that anxiety occurs when the patient cannot keep his aggressions out of consciousness?"

"We are German," the visiting professor countered, "and we are at war. We do not wish to keep aggression out of consciousness."

There was never a cure for these young soldiers, little that could be done. Their symptoms could be expected to last a lifetime. Acheson resolved to improve the prognosis. He tried everything: rest, sensory isolation, warm baths, cold baths. Freud thought the anxiety built up because the soldiers' sexual energies could not find a normal outlet, so Acheson initiated a course of masturbation therapy. One patient in particular, a Herr Lanzer, seemed to make some progress after he overcame his initial resistance. But after several months Acheson was forced to conclude that the effects among the test subjects were not significant compared to the self-controls.

Acheson's superior at the hospital dissuaded him from pursuing the technique any further, suggested his time would be better spent with less intractable patients. It was near the end of the war, there were no more reserves, and no one could be spared at the front. The most reasonable approach was to ship the panic patients back to the war where they could confront the source of their fear. The few who survived seemed to improve, but constant battle was not practical as therapy.

Kotzwara's women were different: there was no battlefront, no secure line of retreat. Their minds were the world and annihilation was everywhere. Eventually they could not go out; they could only hide in their homes.

"Housebound," Kotzwara explains. "Agoraphobia."

"Why do you take them to the shopping centre?"

"We like to immerse them in their fears. We call it flooding. Panic patients sometimes respond very well."

"Sink or swim?"

"It's important to face the feared situation. They have agoraphobia, so we take them to the marketplace, the *agora*. Rather nice how it all fits together."

"Yes," Strasser agrees, "nice."

"Shopping is very therapeutic," Kotzwara adds, "and it does give me a chance to pick up a few things."

The shopping centre is deserted at this hour: facades brightly lit but empty inside, like old love, sad now without the self-talk. The patients emerge from the métro as if entering a minefield. They climb the stairs with their hands on their hearts, controlling their breathing, feeling for palpitations that will signal the attack. Like Freud, they walk along the perimeter, avoiding the vast centre court. Far above are the shopping levels, the vast tomb of atrium. At métro level they are archaeology, buried in a manufactory of desire.

"Take it slow, people," Kotzwara calls out. "You're doing fine. The hour will be over before you know it." He turns to Strasser. "They're always on guard, always watching. Can you feel it? Waves of tension. Vigilance, intuition, primitive radar. They're barely keeping it together."

The only thing open at this hour is a coffee shop. Strasser sets up by the window so Kotzwara can keep an eye on his patients roaming the shopping centre.

"We can speak freely in here," Kotzwara explains. "No one in the group drinks coffee. Too stimulating."

"Another trigger?"

"You're getting the hang of this, Mr. Strasser."

Camera rolling, speed…

"How long have you been doing this, Doctor?"

"Ten years. Not exclusively panic, you understand. My field of interest is sexual disorders, paraphilias—a little more outré. Of course, there are all sorts of lovely connections between sex and panic."

"Can you explain that?"

"There has been some suggestion that the fear response can become eroticized. I don't know if I'd try to explain that. Let's just say that all of these deviances play out on the same stage."

"I would have thought it would all be separate," Strasser suggests. "Different plumbing."

"Plumbing?" Kotzwara asks flatly.

"Hardware."

Kotzwara shakes his head vigorously. "It's not about structures anymore, connections. You have to look at what's driving the connections. It's not about the information flow. It's about the flow itself."

The signal strength of neurotransmitters. Receptors turned off or on or simply fluctuating; amplitude, frequency modulating with chemicals of love, hate, dreams. Each chemical interacting with a single, specialized receptor. A lock and key, male and female, the Transmitter and the Other. The trick was to find out what fitted where, because the combinations were almost limitless, from alpha to omigod.

"We're trying to uncover all those powerful forces working underneath the surface: mood, arousal, anxiety. They're the universal constants, the *abc*, the quantum mechanics of consciousness." Kotzwara sips his café au lait and dabs at the foam clinging to his goatee. "Heady stuff."

He quarter-turns and studies one of his patients rocking back and forth on an atrium bench, sighs. Strasser sharpens the focus as Kotzwara turns back to the camera. "We only have this poor thing to work with," he says, rat-a-tating on his forehead as if sending a message in Morse code. "The ol' conk. *Le cerveau, il faut le sauter.*' Now who said that?" He shrugs and turns back to the camera. "The symptoms we produce—guilt, sad visions, pathetic delusions of grandeur—are so limited. It can be rather a grind."

"But things have changed so much in the past hundred years," Strasser offers. "All the drugs we keep hearing about—Haldol, Prozac." He flounders for a second, then says, "I don't know."

"I dunno," Kotzwara muses. "Yes, that's rather good. Always looking for new monikers. We might use that."

Strasser presses on. "There's been a revolution. Treating insanity, making people feel better about themselves." He's working up to an intro with Dr. Werther Acheson, one of the century's true pioneers. "Wouldn't you say, Doctor, that advances in psychiatry have been among the greatest achievements in the twentieth—"

"Greatest?" Kotzwara smiles paternally. "You may want to pull back, son, broaden your focus. We've made some progress, but there have been setbacks. Medicine isn't a monolith. There are all sorts of specialties, subspecialties, factions, splinter groups arguing about what's right or wrong. Some doctors going down blind alleys with big plans and bad ideas."

"Like quacks?" Strasser asks, thinking maybe he can make this into something. "Faith healers?"

"I was thinking of chiropractors."

"Let's stick to your own profession." Strasser figures he can goad the doctor into gabbing. "Psychiatrists labouring to uncover the mystery of the mind, that sort of thing. If you could comment…?"

Kotzwara stares across at a haberdashery, holds for a hundred frames, adjusts his tie. "The mystery," he says finally to the camera, "is that such complex behaviour can come from just a handful of organizing principles: arousal, sex, humiliation, survival. The brain is finite, Mr. Strasser. It disappoints me. We see that in the mental illnesses. With any complex system so much can go wrong. But really, the symptoms aren't limitless. We share the same moods and delusions and paranoias. Aliens interfere with us, voices whisper in our dreams. When we obsess, it's about dirt or religion or our own feces. We hear the same voices—the Devil or Jesus or the man next door. Only the medium changes. People used to hear Satan whispering over their shoulder. In the sixties the delusions were about Communists or men from outer space taking over their minds."

"And now?"

Kotzwara sips noisily at his coffee. "Thought broadcasting: TV, CNN, the Internet, corporations controlling the medium and the message, messages beamed via satellite and distorting our view of the world. Your bailiwick, I believe."

"You use media," Strasser counters. "I saw you watching movies with your group in the auditorium yesterday."

"Those sessions are a leftover, frankly," Kotzwara says easily. "Not very targeted to symptoms, if you know what I mean."

"Why do you get involved?"

"It keeps the old man happy. A touch of nostalgia. I don't suppose it does any harm. Ask him about it sometime. The movies made Dr. Acheson's career."

EIGHT

Strasser is in front of a music store watching junk TV, the monitors tuned to CFIB with some old black-and-white documentary on the *Hindenburg*. Cheap footage from the archives, something easily repackaged. Onscreen the visuals are grainy, early Led Zeppelin cover art, drag ropes dangling like a cartoon fuse, another couple of seconds and she's going to blow. Back at the station it would be newsman pornography: the airship erect, defying gravity, inflated with the will to power...tension building, waiting for the digitally remastered announcer in New Jersey to start moaning. "It's terrible, it's terrible, it's one of the worst catastrophes of the world..." The newscaster's fantasy of the end of the world.

When the screaming starts, it catches Strasser by surprise, and it's impossible to locate the source in the atrium acoustics. Someone calls out "Ondine!" and he spots Kotzwara jogging grimly through the food court. In the far distance the patients have gathered in front of a drugstore window, as if waiting for a Midnight Madness sale.

Strasser trucks across the mall, easily laps Kotzwara, giving him enough time to set up before the doctor arrives on the scene. He locks down and focuses on a young woman rocking in front of the window, banging her head against the plate glass. The noise is rhythmic, megabass, her forehead getting red, bruising, bleeding. She screams: tuneless, crazy. She starts clutching at her clothes, rips off her sweater, tears at the buttons on her blouse. It is good video.

A shadow appears. Kotzwara steps in front of the lens. "It's all right, Ondine. Practise your breathing. Take it slow. In, out, in, out."

His voice is calm, reassuring. Ondine steps back from the window, the red sponge marks on the glass. Her eyes are moons, the apertures wide open. The veins in her neck bulge. Her temples seem to throb with the pressure of thoughts running wild. The doctor hands her a pill. "It'll be better soon. Just a few more minutes." Kotzwara dabs at the blood on her forehead with a napkin as the other patients look on, keeping a respectful distance, as if they were tinder watching a brushfire. "Keep breathing. It will pass."

And it does pass. It is there on tape. As Strasser watches, Ondine begins to breathe more slowly. He can see the fear leaving her and returning to that other place.

Kotzwara helps the young woman to her feet. "Are you all right now?" She nods, but her face is strangely poised as she looks vaguely toward the camera. Strasser recognizes her from the auditorium, the expression no longer blank but haunted now. Eyes like a daguerrotype of the dead, the eyes capturing the vision of death in a neural pattern, a final photograph of the end of the world. He wants to speak to her, sees her hand almost reaching out to him as Kotzwara leads her to the elevator and métro level.

NINE

The year is 1919. Winter misery, the linden trees stripped bare like raw nerves. Freud hadn't started thinking about what he'd call *Schreck*, the free-floating anxiety only now hatching, earthbound, not yet taking flight.

Onscreen it is there like a distant star, the images still visible from eighty years ago. A great ship, the *Demeter*, crosses the Black Sea, slips through the Dardanelles where the British had met a terrible defeat only a few years before. But the film displays an even earlier time: *May 18, 1838. Panic on board—Mate out of his mind—Rats in the hold…*

The ship presses on, through the Mediterranean, heading north to Ultima Thule. When it docks at Bremen, they are all dead: captain, crew, passengers. Even the cargo is missing: coffins filled with soil from the Carpathians, alive with vermin.

The rats enter the town carrying plague. They invade the houses and infect the inhabitants. An infant dies. A doctor marks a cross in chalk on the door. The townspeople panic. They try to flee. But it is too late. Something has arrived in Europe and taken root in Demeter's cornfields razed by war. A sickness, an idea. An intuition of death.

⊕

The war for soldiers was a *Ladenkino*, flickering kinetoscope images of no man's land, *canardeurs* sniping in a graveyard of trees, the screaming of bombs, the bullet shriek of rats underfoot in the trench.

"The films," Strasser says. "Tell me about them."

"What do you know?"

"There was a screening yesterday at the hospital. *Casablanca*."

"I used to enjoy the films very much," Acheson says.

"It was more than that. A nurse called it film therapy. Dr. Kotzwara—"

"You have spoken with him?"

"This morning. He said the movies gave you your start."

After the war the hospitals were filled. Trauma cases, amnesia, shell shock, soldier's heart. "The mind anchors the world in place with an idea, Mr. Strasser. But if the idea fails, if that mooring is torn away or lost, the mind begins to drift." Out beyond the shallows, losing its course, unable to return home.

"Each of these men held a story, terrible in its simplicity. For them, the complexity, the fine beliefs, the rich emotion that lingers on the palate—" he pauses to press his fingertips to his lips "—they are lies, delusions."

"And the movies?"

"More delusion," Acheson says. "But we must rebuild a person's faith, give him new stories to believe in. You are thinking this is crude, yes? You cannot fill a man's mind with pictures on a screen."

"Did it work?"

Acheson smiles. "Good. You are like me—a pragmatist."

It began as an experiment after the war. Every week Acheson would take his patients out of the hospital to the cinema. The film *Nosferatu* was an early success, the men appearing calmer after seeing it, less agitated. The lurid sex films during those Weimar years were too stimulating, and it was soon apparent to Acheson that the selection of movies was crucial. The clinical logic of Detective Webbs, the German Sherlock Holmes, produced no response; the patients did not understand the order of his world. A few improved after watching horror films, as if in *Der Andere*, *Golem*, or *Homunculus* they saw themselves: doomed creatures arising from the trenches as men of clay. Soulless: *cheated out of the greatest thing life has to offer*.

The therapeutic value lay in the *projection*, seeing a larger-than-life image of the inner horror. Here the stories were writ large: the stern Junker father forcing the son into the war, the frightened boy turning coward in battle and bringing shame to the family. In the kinolight there was catharsis more real than the violence outside the cinema: political demonstrations, loud voices on the radio, beer-hall putsches. The chaos was contained just as their symptoms—the night sweats and fear visions—might one day be controlled.

Change tapes.

Another anecdote: Frankfurt just before the end of the war. Acheson was employed at the Ward for War Neuroses. One night he heard someone weeping in the washing-up room. He saw a figure huddled in the corner. A man in his late thirties, taut with tension, was smoking nervously. As he dragged on the cigarette, he cupped his hand, shielding the glowing tip so he would not be a target. One of many habits that perseverated from the trenches.

"Herr Lanzer?" It was Ernst Lanzer, who had regressed after Acheson had cancelled his group masturbation therapy sessions. "Are you ill?"

"There is an odour. A bad smell."

Acheson remembered there was a dripping sound from one of the water closets, a cistern cracked or overflowing. "Let us go back to the ward. The air is foul in here. The pipes are old."

"Not the pipes, Doctor. The air. It is dying."

It was a common delusion in such cases. Many of the war-neurosis patients could not remove themselves from trench life, the stink of putrefaction, shit, mustard gas. The rot was in the brain. Acheson was still new to his medical training, but he understood the phenomenon. His own mind detected odours in the moments preceding an epileptic attack. During the petit mal, his thoughts became blank as if a hand were smoothing out the worried fissures and trenches of his brain. A minute, an hour passed, then he returned.

"Where were you?"

"It was a dark place like the bottom of a cooking pot. There were explosions. I could hear someone shouting. There was a dug-out section of the trench where we kept ammunition. I tried to push through the opening, but the walls collapsed." Lanzer began to sob quietly. "I was trapped. I couldn't get away. I could hear them coming."

"And then?"

Herr Lanzer could not continue.

Dr. Acheson gestures to stop the camera, asks for a drink of water. "He was a very disturbed man, Herr Lanzer. A sexual obsessive, rather prone to episodes of violence. They began to visit the Bufa tents, Lanzer seemingly energized as they pushed through the flap into the darkness as if entering a cave. He especially enjoyed the hygiene films released by the Gesellschaft zur Bekämpfung der Geschlechtskrankheiten, the Society for Combatting Venereal Diseases. Scores of films were produced: *Let There Be Light*, *Germinating Life*, you understand. Other films were not so enlightening. *Hyänen der Lust*; *Aus eines Mannes Mädchenjahren*; *Frauen, die der Abgrund verschlingt*."

"I don't understand."

"*Hyenas of Lust*," Acheson explains. "*A Man's Maidenhood* was a sordid story of homosexual inversion, a certain anality in Herr Lanzer's obsessions. *Women Engulfed by the Abyss* purported to warn the men about prostitution, but it stimulated them to the opposite effect. I remember Lanzer particularly enjoyed scenes with rats in them, in the tenements, in the sin holes and streets. They were symbolic, of course."

"How long did you treat him?" Strasser asks.

"Not so very long—a few months. I was a medical student. It was not my responsibility. There was little we could do in such cases. How do you treat war? When the fighting began, some men were not prepared. The mind is weak. Lanzer's tendency to abuse himself did not make matters better. But it is true that he was calmer after the movies. It was a beginning, you see. I started to feel hope for these men. It might be possible through some intervention to force the mind to change."

"With movies?"

"At first, yes."

The cinema offered a respite for men who needed to be exorcised of the spirit that had invaded them, an intuition, an unreal sense of this nightmarish life. They were possessed by the Uncanny, *das Unheimliche*, as Freud called it that autumn. The mind was an all-powerful being that could annihilate with a thought. The gods, said Freud, had turned into demons.

"Was this Herr Lanzer cured?"

"I would say so, yes," Acheson says. "Certainly he was functional and we could not afford to have him malinger. He was returned to the front. I believe he did not dislike the trenches—a primitive, cloacal environment. His obsession proved fatal, I'm afraid. He was killed just before the armistice."

TEN

She is there in playback: half-turned, a strand of black hair jagged across her too-white face. As she looks at him, her expression is what an alienist of the last century might have called *la belle indifférence*. Ondine seems almost to reach out to him as she is led away.

Strasser looks up from the viewfinder, spots the Institute's research director slipping along the perimeter of the lobby. "Do you have a few minutes, Dr. Baum?" he asks quickly as he intercepts him. "For the piece on Dr. Acheson. Is there some place we can talk?"

"This place was built on talk," Dr. Baum whispers, eyeing the dome as if it's a satellite dish reading his thoughts. There is no reaction from Strasser, so he begins to explain the joke. Freud, Jung, the talking cure: they are bronzed *lares*, house gods in an agnostic age. No one talks about talk anymore.

"Very good, Doctor," Strasser says, shifting the camera onto his other shoulder, "but I'm a little short on time. Is there someplace we can go? I understand you've been here since the beginning, when Dr. Acheson started up the Institute."

"Who told you that?"

"It was in a press release. Dr. Acheson couldn't give me all the details about the early days—"

"Is that what he talked about?"

"Growing up in Germany, his father. He mentioned a patient."

"Who?"

"A Herr Lanzer?"

Baum nods curtly. "Ernst Lanzer. An early success. Psychological therapy. It was a poke in the eye for Freud, who'd treated Lanzer about ten years before. Made a complete hash of it. Of course it's all physiology now: neurons, synapses, brain chemicals. The stuff bubbling away in the old crock."

They enter a breezeway connecting the main building to an old brick home left over from the turn of the century, pass through anterooms, cotillion suites, a grand ballroom with fluted mouldings and wainscoting intricate as a wiring diagram. The charm of Edwardian excess, a world so much saner in its mad way than it was destined to become.

"This is the Institute proper," Baum says, "what we call the Psychopharm." The rooms are an interconnecting hive of labs, activity fuelled with research grants and drug company money. "When I started, they were still performing insulin shock." Young Turk days. He'd done his share of slogging down to the stockyards to scrounge insulin from animal pancreases. Back on the wards, the patients would moan at the first prick of the needle, then get the sweats as they went into shock, eyes fixed on the no man's land ahead. What did they see as they plummeted down, down, down past the mezzanine to the basement and subbasement of consciousness? What lay in the darkness tinged blood-red? There on the river of sweat was Charon, pallid, mouth stuffed with candy bars, waves of unconscious lapping on the shore as rats scuttled in the recesses…

Strasser pauses beside a laboratory bench and dumps his gear. They are deep underground in the research section: grim cinder-block walls and greenish fluorescent light. Baum leads him into a small bunker. The walls are blinding white tile, a bugger to light.

"What's that noise?" Strasser asks.

At the far end of the room is a videowall of rats scree-screeing in cages. "This is where we do some of our experimental work," Baum explains. "You can set up your camera over there. It should make for some pretty pictures while we talk."

Strasser does a quick pan across the room, slow zoom on Baum as he crosses to one of the cages and picks out a bigger specimen. It's a sewer rat, Norwegian variety, already prepped, skull shaved. Baum puts on gloves and efficiently injects the animal in the belly with a hypo cartoonishly long. "This little beggar," he says, gesticulating with the flaccid body, "bit me the other day through my gauntlet." He plucks off a glove to demonstrate, then sucks at his thumb, a thin web of saliva dangling and catching the video light when he pulls it out of his mouth. "Not that he knows. Their memory is quite rudimentary."

The camera is locked down on the tripod and running. "When did you first meet Dr. Acheson?" Strasser asks.

"After the war. I had been training with Wilder Penfield's people aboard the HMS *Mal de Mer*." He pauses for an effect that doesn't come. "Sort of a swing device that Penfield set up to test G-forces, war neurosis, sea sickness."

"Right."

It was the 1940s and the psychiatric profession had been undistinguished until then, not quite passing muster scientifically speaking. Quack cures, Bedlam, sterilizing the mentally defective. "The war changed that," Baum explains. "We were needed, you see. The powers that be were recruiting like mad, but they had a problem. A sizable number of the chaps—one-fifth—didn't make it past the mental screening. Imagine that: thousands of our fighting men were too disturbed to kill Nazis. For the first time people started to think that maybe something was going on, something they needed to investigate.

They had to come to us, you see. We became quite flush. The government couldn't give us research money fast enough. The boom kept on even after '45. We had to make people sane if we were going to be ready for World War III."

"And Dr. Acheson?"

"He arrived a year later. Impressive credentials, of course. Word got around that he was recruiting, planning to set up an institute."

"Where did the money come from?"

Baum shrugs. "You don't inquire about that sort of thing. It is usually best not to ask how someone earns his living. It starts you thinking about what people are prepared to do for money."

Work got under way within a year. Baum, a resident at the time, was hired as a research assistant. The profession was split between neurology and psychiatry, structure and phenomenon, and Baum had been in a professional quandary about the direction he should take. His mind was open; he could have gone either way. Dr. Acheson changed that. The man was an inspiration. When they first met, Baum had expected Acheson to be interested in psychological theories: Freud, Jung, the mind of *mittelEurope*. But Acheson was emphatically modern. The man had gone American, claimed the profession was now a matter of biology, economics. Of course, he despised Freud, called him a respectable scientist who had ended up chasing dreams. Acheson wanted to reverse all of that, erase the past, make the profession a science. During rounds his questions to the residents were always the same: What were the signs? What was the cause? How could the situation be changed?

The scientific approach meant research, new drugs, money. It wasn't a very romantic prospect, and Baum—young, naive—had resisted at first. The whole business seemed somewhat crass, truth be told. What had Freud called it: "the chase after money, position, reputation." But Acheson was persuasive, could quote from memory Freud's 1924 paper on the economic problem of masochism. Even Herr Freud had conceded that money—the *transaction*—lay at the heart of the psychoanalytic process.

Dr. Baum frowns as he lays out the rat prone on a table, body limp spaghetti. He fiddles with the screws on the stereotaxic cage to position the head just so. A thin trace of blood runs out of the rat's ears, too graphic even for TV.

"That doesn't hurt them?" Strasser asks. "The eardrums, I mean."

"Breaks them completely, I'm afraid, but they grow back. Not that there'll be time. We sacrifice the animal when the experiment's done."

"The rats don't sense that?"

"They have no fear. They don't know what's going to happen, not like we do. We can anticipate, plan, foresee the future. That's our greatest advantage over the animals. It's also our greatest curse." He nods sharply to Strasser. "Ready for the close-up."

Strasser is too slow to catch Baum reaching for a scalpel among the tools lined up on a towel. But he is there for the incision, scalp splitting into a blood-welling *I*, peeling back the skin to expose the bone.

"You can see bregma here," Baum tells the camera, pointing at a crease in the skull. The doctor flips a switch. A miniature drill with a conical bit like a roof ventilator starts to whine into the bone. Strasser angles the camera as a neat dime-shaped hole is formed, dark as an oubliette. The doctor is tense, all business now, pupils narrowed to rat's eyes under the high-intensity lights. "The procedure today is to lesion a portion of the brain anatomy using a radiofrequency cauterizer. Afterward we test the subject to find out what deficits we have produced."

"Is that necessary?"

"We need to understand the structures being manipulated when we research new compounds."

Baum lowers a needle electrode into the brainjelly, but Strasser stops him. He wants to zoom to a tight close-up of the cortex, the first time he has seen a living brain. He imagines ideas running underground beneath the tiny pattern of fissures, wet with humours, seepage, groundwater, in the sewerwork of cranium.

"All right, can we try that again?" Strasser asks.

Baum appears irritated but raises the needle and starts again. On the far wall the living mural of caged rats shrieks in chorus. "This electrode is placed at a selected spot in the brain. When we turn on the current, the tip of the electrode heats up like a toaster element." He lowers the needle again and flicks a switch. It is over in a second. "It's a simple method, reverse-engineering the brain, Mr. Strasser. Information by ablation. We learn from what we destroy."

ELEVEN

"I'm Robert Strasser. You're Ondine, aren't you?"

"You were at the shopping centre this morning."

"With Dr. Kotzwara, yes."

"Someone said you were doing a documentary."

"A biography. *Notable Lives*, on Dr. Acheson."

"I heard he was dead."

"Not yet. I want the piece to show how he got started, set up the Institute, that sort of thing. I'm going to profile his ideas, his work, some of the things he's accomplished."

She looks him over, the bulk of camera, the newsman trench coat. "I saw him once, an old guy."

"He's still old."

"Funny thing to say."

"Is it?"

"Still old?" she repeats, a hint of hostility maybe, but Strasser doesn't catch her drift. "That's all you've learned so far?"

"No major revelations, if that's what you mean."

"You're going to mention the movies? And the shopping centre?"

"If it helps explain the story."

"In other words, all the wacky shit. I thought so." She turns to leave.

"It isn't like that."

"Isn't it?"

He tries to work up a little charm. "Maybe if you helped me. I figured if I did pickup interviews with various people at the Institute, put things into context…"

"You're saying this interview's a pickup?" She catches him off guard, seems to enjoy that. "How did you find me?"

"I heard him say he was seeing you this afternoon. I followed you."

"And you filmed me. When I had my attack."

"It's all part of the story."

"Don't you need some kind of permission for that?"

"I'll give you a waiver."

"No."

"Just a piece of paper to sign."

"No."

"Is there someplace we can talk? Maybe you could tell me a bit about yourself."

They go to an off-campus coffee shop, but Ondine doesn't let him bring the video equipment inside. "We're just going to talk, right?" she asks.

"Sure. A conversation."

"You make it sound old-fashioned. But if we're just talking, I don't want a record. I don't want anything showing up on TV or getting beamed into outer space. How do I know what you'll do with the tape? Maybe you'll load it onto the Internet for all the freaks to watch."

The coffee shop is harshly lit like a display case, an Edward Hopper joint noisy with clatter. "What do you do?" Strasser asks. "Work?"

"Student."

"Aren't you a little old to be in school?"

"Are you always blunt, or do you tell yourself you're being honest?"

"It's the job. I get so focused on the story, on getting all the facts, that I forget everything else." He smiles apologetically. "I had to ask."

"No, you didn't, but it's a good excuse."

Strasser isn't going to mikewallace her; ambush journalism doesn't always work and he is, well, a pragmatist. So he takes it slow, drawing Ondine out. He'll settle for a few details, videocaptures he can string together into a story later.

She shrugs and forces a smile. "I would have finished my post-grad by now. Things got in the way."

Meaning her illness, Strasser knows, some kind of breakdown. "What were you studying?"

"History. The Beothuks. Shawnadithit."

Strasser comes up empty. It isn't a name he's come across on any of the TV stations.

"Shawnadithit was a woman in the Beothuk tribe in Newfoundland. I was trying to collect some information on her."

"How? Interviews? Man-on-the-street?"

"The tribe is extinct."

"Any stock footage?"

"This was almost two hundred years ago. You know, before there were cameras."

"Gotcha," Strasser says.

She had been researching for months but hadn't accomplished much. Not at the university, nor with any of the other sources she had tried. If there were records, they were prelanguage: in the wind and soil, in the blank rune of Newfoundland.

Shortly after the turn of the nineteenth century it became apparent to government authorities that the war against the Indian had been won. The Natives' migration routes, their patterns of behaviour—the seacoast for the summer fishing, inland for the winter hunt—were unchangeable, and yet it had been years since anyone had encountered a redskin. Something in the air had shifted, the spirits had gone to another place. In St. John's the local magistrate, John Bland, offered a bounty of £100 for the capture of any living Beothuk.

During the winter, Shawnadithit, her mother, and her sister kept to the interior where the snow was deep and it was safe. But deep snow also made it impossible to hunt, and they had no boat to cross over to the island where auks laid their eggs. The three women subsisted on blue mussels and birchbark, but they grew weak and gaunt. It was clear they would soon die of starvation and nostalgia for how life with the tribe had been.

As the ground thawed, Shawnadithit dug shallow trenches for their beds and laid a fire at the centre, the flames low so the smoke would not alert the white man. Her mother attended Shawnadithit's sister, who coughed often now, speckling the snow with blood. It had come to an end. As Shawnadithit lay down, she could see through the vent in the *mammateek* the half-moon *kuis*, stranded in the sky like a forgotten rune. If it was a prophecy, she did not understand. The shaman was dead and there was no one to read the sign. The world was mute. The starless sky was a shroud. The trench was a grave.

She arose, made a thin soup from berries and grass, and stared into the fire. The smoke in the firelight was a screen on which Shawnadithit could see the future. She had heard in the creation myths common to Beothuk and *buggishaman* alike of how it was destined to be. Her people had come here across a bridge of ice and with the winter they had all returned to that place. Now as the bridge melted she could taste their tears. But she could not cross over. She was stranded here far from the land of death.

⊕

"I could have worked longer that day, but I was supposed to meet someone in the afternoon," Ondine tells Strasser in the coffee shop.

"Who?"

"That doesn't matter."

It was December, there was snow on the ground. The view over the city was beautiful, almost painful. The light soft at that hour, red-tinged aura. But that is how they always describe it: the prodrome.

"It started then," he asks, "the panic?" Ondine doesn't respond; she's on rerun. "You've never gone back?"

"I go back all the time."

"You know what I mean. Your thesis."

"I lost confidence, Mr. Strasser."

"Robert."

She can see he's trying, but how to explain? Her genetics are fucked, all the fear, the imbalances in her brain, everything beginning and ending in the genes. Every deviance like a point mutation, her chromosomal X a cross hair for the shit coming down. "These interviews with Dr. Acheson. Do you think you can re-create someone's life?"

"I just put the facts together," Strasser says.

"What if there are no facts, just things people tell you? What if you can't trust what they say? Even you have to question your sources. The only reports about Shawnadithit are from white men. The information's tainted."

"You can still put the pieces together. S'like a jigsaw."

"What if there is no picture? What if you don't understand what you're seeing?"

"We're talking TV, not brain surgery. If you ask me, it sounds like you've been working this Shawnadithit thing and you haven't been able to come up with the story."

"You don't understand."

"That's your job. Make me understand."

"I can't." She gets up and collects her purse.

"I want to see you again."

She is surprised at the urgency in his voice, angered. "You got me marked out, a big *X* on my forehead? You got a thing for sick chicks and you figure I'm fucked up enough to go along with it?"

"It's not like that. I thought if we talked…"

"Are you talking or interviewing? It's not the same thing." She turns away, tired of the conversation, tired of Strasser. "Go back to work. What I told you wasn't anything special. It was just stories, Mr. Strasser, talk. Stuff people say to each other when the cameras are off."

TWELVE

After the attack on the mountain in 1989, Ondine had remained in her apartment for days, feeling little, thinking nothing. She wasn't alone: the television stayed on day and night, the voices chattering news from the front lines. She drifted, unable to focus, dozing on the couch and awakening confused, thoughts of doom melding with meteorology, sky falling like snow.

She unplugged the TV, got the name of a doctor from a friend of a guy, booked an appointment with Emil Kotzwara.

"We've set up a canopy apparatus to test your breathing, your sensitivity to CO2."

Kotzwara reproduced her symptoms in pornographic detail— heart racing to the top of the ridge, breast heaving, breath shredding in the thin air. He noted her reactions, drizzle of sweat on her breastbone, shudder of nipple, breasts rising as she gripped the armrests. Her memories were leaden grey, heavy as winter sky, which Kotzwara colourized: waves of terror in sea-green eyes, white teeth biting blood-red lips. If there was something unsettling in the way he observed her, Ondine didn't care. He was a medium calling forth the poltergeist in the attic and sending him packing, if only for a while.

She tried to keep working despite the depression that stalked her. She read books, monographs, newspapers from the 1820s—anything that might somehow lead her to Shawnadithit—but she found it difficult to concentrate. Her brain was weary with information. All she could capture was a mood, an aura, like a migraine about to descend.

"What do you see?"

"A tower."

"What time is it?"

"I don't know. Five. Five-thirty."

He wanted to know if something had occurred when Ondine was five, five and a half. The hour on the clock face was her age, you see, something Freud had said.

"No, nothing I remember."

"No recall of an accident, trauma, molestation?"

"No."

"Interesting."

She continued to see Kotzwara but adopted alternative information flows: bibliomancy, the omens in objects found in garbage cans, antique shops, at the side of the road. She read her horoscope. She cast runes—*Mannaz, Perth, Nauthiz*—all reversed. She was lost, blocked, uncertain where to turn.

On the mountain after the attack she had lost faith. She had believed there was an orderly world—documented, rational, capable of being analyzed—but that was before. Her totems were clay pigeons and she felt herself falling into the cross hairs.

Then she had a revelation. In the spring a lightning storm descended on the mountain like electroshock. The city blacked out. Ondine tuned in the weather report on an old transistor radio, but she couldn't hold its attention, the signal shifting like a bored guest at a party. She fiddled with the dial until she picked up a local phone-in show. "Our lines are down," a voice said on the radio, "so we'll have to do this the old-fashioned way. I want you to feel it. I want you to feel yourself becoming conscious. I'm asking the listeners out there to touch your radio, uncloud your minds. Reach out and feel my voice."

The voice was as cheesy as the Shadow's, and Ondine felt herself starting to smile. It was absurd. But it was the first time she had smiled in a long time. She put her hands on the radio.

"That's it," the Voice encouraged her. "Feel how communication unites us. Don't hear it. Don't think. Don't analyze. *Feel it.*"

She didn't know what it was she was supposed to feel, but she relaxed her mind, tried to be receptive. Then she felt something: a mid-range vibration, a warmth that might have been the transistors overheating. Ondine resolved to track down the talk-show guest. She called the radio station, but the woman she spoke to claimed there was no show that evening because the storm had knocked out the transformer. But there was a psychic on about a year ago, part of a series. No name or address, but the woman thought he worked out of a dump on the Décarie strip. Used a stage name, Bill Mannekin.

Ondine tracked him down to a makeshift office behind an Italian restaurant. "I need your help," she said straight off without introducing herself.

He had her pegged right away, not psychic so much as shrewd; he'd been around. She was the type who wouldn't tell him her name; he was expected to know.

"Of course, have a seat," Mannekin said amiably, his voice a disappointing half octave higher in real life than on radio. He was small, undistinguished, with a greasy handlebar moustache. When she settled herself across from him, he said, "I see the number seven. Is that your name?" He felt her resistance.

"Ondine," she said, correcting him.

Mannekin nodded. "I was, of course, speaking numerologically. *Shevah*. You are a philosopher, but also a recluse."

"I'm a student."

"Do you have ID?"

She flushed as if caught trying to buy beer underage. "Why do you want—?"

"Add the numbers. Reduce them to a single digit."

Ondine reluctantly complied. The ID number added up to—why not?—seven. "What does that prove?"

"Seven is a powerful number. Seven sins, seven petitions, seven gifts of the spirit. Seven days of the week. Seven types of light."

"Lucky seven," she countered. "7-Eleven."

"You understand," Mannekin replied, apparently deaf to sarcasm. "It is a glyph, half of a triangle."

"I'm a historian. I don't believe—"

"Hitler's Party card was number seven."

She may have started to respect him then, his unforced irony, his slippery ease in working her. Even if it was only a con, at least he made the effort. He cared enough to do that.

"All right," Ondine said, tugging a cigarette pack out of her purse as if preparing to wait out a siege, "what can you tell me?"

Mannekin bummed a smoke, studied her in the match flare. She wasn't a true believer, not a skeptic, not lovelorn, not a kid on a bet. There was a darkness in her Lilith eyes, a crystal ball unplumbed. "You're a struggling soul, Ondine. You remind me of someone. A woman."

"Your wife?"

"This woman is dead. It was a long time ago. History was tired. It was winding down. It happens sometimes. Strands of history become so strained by the past that they break. The time line ends."

"And then?"

"Time is a wave. It drowns everything. It drowned her."

"Who was she?"

"Her name was Shawnadithit."

⊕

So it began, Ondine's search for Shawnadithit that would take her into the Beothuk spiritual essence, there to greet Shawna's

Otherworld opposite, her doppelganger, a woman with raven hair who shies from the *bahir* light, not quite ready to be interviewed…

The process would take time. Ondine had too many years of academia behind her to believe readily in anything. Mannekin wasn't concerned, merely bided his time. He confided in her, offered embarrassing facts about himself, established a certain level of trust. "I realize these aren't the most impressive surroundings," he said. "As a businessman, I'm a bit of a bust. I used to make ends meet entertaining the kiddies at the restaurant—the Italian place you passed on your way in. Family dining. Magic tricks. Severed hands, talking skulls."

"No good?"

"I got canned. The black arts were a little too dark for Mom and Dad. It was no Happyland."

He rummaged underneath the table, pulled out a kewpie doll. "This is my new sideline." It was a plastic doll decked out in Hong Kong's version of Native American dress. "Not much to look at, but the selling point's the hair," he explained. "It's real. I still have one or two contacts in the cosmetics trade." Meaning funeral parlours, colleagues who prepared bodies for those open-casket affairs, the hair growing even after death so nobody cared if a few locks went missing. Mannekin niche-marketed the dolls to mourners, each one certified that the hair had belonged to the loved one.

Ondine felt queasy. "Touch it," he urged. "Feel the hair."

"I don't want to."

"This one is special. The hair is Beothuk. I didn't ask where it came from—a museum, a scalp taken by one of the colonists. I don't know. Maybe it comes from Shawnadithit herself. It's the only thing that's left. There are no artifacts, personal accounts. Just the hair."

"It can't be hers."

"Touch it."

Ondine sensed that Mannekin was challenging her. She felt annoyed. There was no goddamn way he was going to get the better of her. She touched the hank of hair. She worked the doll head as if it were a worry bead.

"Good," Mannekin said. "The dolls help people remember." He smiled at her with yellow teeth. "Lives are memories, but you know that."

Memories that slip away, leaving only a thin trace like hair oil on the fingers.

THIRTEEN

D r. Acheson leaves a message for Strasser to meet him at the chalet on the mountain. Strasser finds the doctor on the terrace overlooking the park, with its late-season strollers, the distraction of trees turning fiery red. In profile he is a hawk spying his quarry a mile distant.

"Good. You have come, Mr. Strasser."

"It wouldn't have been more convenient in your office?"

"I admire scenery, action. The epic. Even for *Kulturfilme*."

"Is there some special reason why you wanted to meet here?"

Acheson savours the air as if the mountain were purifying the city smog. *"Der Heilige Berg."*

"Is that another one of your movies?"

"I was thinking of the book. I admired it very much. In it a man says that the Americans, the English, the Swiss climb mountains for sport. But not the Germans. Why they climb he does not know. But it is not for sport."

"The last time we spoke you talked about the movies."

"Movies," Acheson says distastefully. "You understand, I do not speak of Hollywood, those films about unfortunates with terrible secrets that we must discover—*Three Faces of Eve, The Prince of Tides*. No. A doctor is not a detective. We do not restore the mind like puzzle pieces. My approach was strictly therapeutic—to expose my patients to novel stimuli to see if they would respond. This was science. It was very hard. Lanzer was the first—promising but perhaps too far gone. We tried different techniques, yet the progress was not good. I am a capable doctor, but they did not always improve. The circumstances demanded more radical techniques."

"Such as?"

Acheson gestures for Strasser to cut. New setup.

They will try again, but Acheson will direct the scene. Strasser will stand at the base of the stairs as the doctor gloriaswansons down the steps from the chalet terrace. He will talk about a breakthrough in therapy, a new idea that was destined to change the course of his career.

Rolling…

"We had gone to the Ufa Palace in Berlin. I remember the air was warm. It must have been spring. Before the elections, you understand."

He had hoped that one of Renata Muller's films would be playing, but all of Berlin that season was talking about *Das Blaue Licht*, what is called *The Blue Light*. The film had only opened the month before and had immediately won favour from the critics. Acheson had grown weary of the mountain films. In the end he managed, despite it being the last minute, to obtain a dozen tickets, said to be worth a small fortune on the black market.

The picture that night was unlike the other berg films the men had seen. In truth they did not respond well to stories about men climbing mountains, struggling, perhaps falling to their death. Stories of mountaineers, the tired structures of conflict, rivalry, two men competing for the same woman. One falls from a precipice. He dangles from a rope that even now is fraying. He is moments from death. Will his rival pull him to safety? That was the genre then. Those were the stories that were told.

That night was different. The star was Leni Riefenstahl: blonde, magnificent, artful in her Gypsy rags. In the story she played Junta, a witch who lived alone on Mount Cristallo, a magical place bathed in a blue light. Junta understood the pulsing, cerulean soul lying buried in the mountain. But her lover, an artist, betrayed her as artists will do. He revealed the secret. The mysterious blue light, the *nogah* glow, emanated from crystals as precious as radium. So the people of the village stole the crystals, and little Leni, no longer able to use their light as her guide, fell from the mountain to her death.

For Acheson this sentimental fairy tale was a revelation. The men—their mood flattened, their minds numbed by memories—responded. A few wept openly. Over the next few months of therapy they spoke of nothing else. Could the doctor arrange a meeting with this actress, Fraulein Riefenstahl? Just a few moments? Perhaps they could take a coffee?

One patient, Freudlose, a former infantryman, saw the film sixty-two times. He confessed to Acheson that he was in love with Junta.

"You understand that this woman, this Gypsy character, is not real?" Acheson said.

The patient knew it was only a film, but it made no difference. Acheson understood: the reality of the woman did not matter. It was enough for Freudlose to pass a few hours in the dark, imagining a life on the mountain with Junta. During that time, he did not feel afraid.

"But he was deluded, wasn't he?" Strasser asks.

"It did not matter. Should we be concerned how a man's spirit is restored, where he drinks his fill of hope? Freudlose's symptoms improved. There was objective evidence. He began to function well. He later fell in love with a young woman from Munich. They married and had two sons. By all accounts, he was a good husband and father. Some of the other men—those without delusions—did not fare so well." Acheson pauses to light a pipe, the smoke a soft focus for the camera lens.

"If you wouldn't mind, Doctor, could you hold the pipe out of the shot?" Strasser asks. "Smoking onscreen may make the program harder to syndicate."

"Like so?"

"That's fine, sir."

"Perhaps you would like a rest? Then we shall walk."

"In a few moments. When you finish the story."

Acheson frowns, puzzled for a moment. "There is nothing more. Herr Freudlose left therapy. We did not see him again."

"You mentioned a breakthrough. A new idea."

"Love." Acheson permits himself a smile. "Is that not a good ending to the story?"

"I don't understand."

"I am modest. I did not cure this patient. Fraulein Riefenstahl did not cure him, although I am sure she would enjoy the credit. No, an emotion—love—cured Freudlose. I am not a sentimentalist. But it is true that emotion can modulate how we think, how we respond to stimuli. The war had altered the structure of these men's minds. A thought occurs. It should go from A to B. But if there is trauma, what happens? This thought begins to twist and turn. It gets lost in the trenches of the mind. Freud believed we should excavate these thoughts. I found a new approach. It was necessary to rechannel the energies, change the way we think. But we could not do this with talk. We needed something more powerful."

"Love?" Strasser says doubtfully.

"You are thinking, perhaps, that my approach is not scientific?"

"Love means different things to different people. It isn't something you can test."

"Everything can be tested. But do not think that we used honeymooners. That is not practical." As he lays out the problem, he jabs at the camera with his pipe stem, as if planning an assault by a platoon of researchers. "This was many years ago. We did not have many tools. We did not understand the brain. As for love, no, we did not understand that at all. We had many arguments. What does this mean, 'falling in love'? A procreative urge? A collection of pleasant associations? Conditioning? No, that was not the way to proceed. There was not enough time for such arguments. There was a need for a simpler approach to attack the problem."

"A shortcut?"

"Just so. Do you agree?"

"How can you analyze something you can't comprehend within a system you don't understand?"

"That is luxury—understanding how something works. It is not necessary. You do not understand your wife, but you know she will cook turnips for dinner."

The comparison strikes Strasser as absurd. "If we could return to the breakthrough, Doctor?"

"You are impatient," Acheson observes, "but you do not see. We do not need to understand how a system works. We only need the power to change it. It is a simple problem. We take a man. He has an illness, he falls in love, and his illness improves. What we call love is a chemical. It can be synthesized, administered. We give this chemical to a second man and his symptoms also improve. It is the same for a third man, and a fourth. They all improve."

"Let me get this straight. For the experiment to work, you would need a drug that would make people feel they were in love."

"Precisely."

"But that isn't possible."

"In the twentieth century, Mr. Strasser," Acheson says mischievously, "everything was possible."

II

The psychologist in the year 2001 will be the master ecstacist.
—Dr. Timothy Leary

Paranoids are the only ones who notice anything anymore.
—Anatole Broyard

ONE

The Engel was in Berlin, off the Charlottenburger Chaussee. There was no sign. A visitor would descend three concrete steps to a black oaken door that was always locked. Most people, those who had heard of the club through word of mouth, were admitted. The entrance fee was twenty marks. There were few restrictions: only politicians, soldiers, members of the auxiliary police were not permitted to disturb the patrons.

There were gossipers, those who disapproved of the club, who claimed that the Engel was *Der Blaue Engel*, a reference to the ruin that befell Emil Jannings in the notorious Marlene Dietrich flick. In truth the Engel was Acheson's belated tribute to his father, to the early days at the E. Merck laboratories when the company had been known as Engel-Apotheke, the apothecary angel. When Acheson turned twenty-one, he was given papers dating back to his father's tenure at Merck, with laboratory notes describing the manufacture of a monoalkyl derivative, sister to amphetamine. The chemical was manufactured as a tonic, a cough syrup with intriguing chemical properties that were only alluded to in the notes.

Acheson skimmed the papers before putting them away, their significance, the wealth of the discovery, remaining as submerged as Rheingold. But no idea—good or ill—is forgotten. Years later at the Wagner festival in Bayreuth, Acheson was seized by an epileptic storm terrifying in its intensity. He regained consciousness a few moments later, lying supine on the ground in postictal collapse. As he stared up at the sun, he saw *zohar*, a benzene radiance, a polygonic aura he believed was a vision. Rolling over, he observed the close-up choreography of ants parading in perfect dressage. In their martial columns there was prescience: these ants communicated with scent trails, a chemical language as primal and occult as the mind itself. Why not humans? Could he not develop a compound that would—like love—touch the mind and alter behaviour?

The solution lay in his father's papers. Acheson Sr. had noted that the new amphetamine compound induced feelings of affection, a collective harmony, a sense of peace. In those anomic postwar years the soul hungered for contact. What was needed was a manufactory of desire.

He described his plan to a few confidants: Professor Chriemhilde from the university; Ernst "Putzi" Hanfstaengl, who apparently discussed the matter with Geli Raubal. Hanfstaengl would later introduce Acheson to Dr. Haushofer, rumoured to be a member of the Vril Society, a group of esoterics, a cult that understood how to operate without scrutiny.

The Engel moved every other month; later it would be every week. The basements it occupied were small, filthy, with concrete walls and low beams. The only light came from candles on the tables, glow softened by tobacco smoke. Food and alcohol were not served. There was no stage. The only music—Lotte Lenya, Marlene Dietrich—came from a gramophone in the corner. There would be a murmur of conversations at the table: muted, punctuated by nervous laughter. But the patrons were not there to be seen. They avoided one another's eyes. They never looked beyond the circle of light on the table.

At precisely eleven o'clock Dr. Acheson would enter. The room hushed as the doctor passed from table to table dispensing small blue pills. The customers received them wordlessly, placing the pills on their tongues and swallowing them with small mouthfuls of water. No one asked questions. No one addressed Acheson. A few may have believed him to be Herr Engel himself.

The ritual completed, Acheson would withdraw to a corner of the room and wait, jotting down notes in a minuscule hand. Within a half hour it would begin: voices became softer, more subdued; eyes focused on a face, a shy smile, a lock of hair. Then a hand would begin that painful passage across a tabletop to feel the warmth of a lover's skin, the soft pressure of a hand's embrace. A small gesture, but there was contact across the no man's land. And the past—its grievances and resentments, harsh words spoken in disappointment and anger—was erased, the chalkboard clean. The runestone was blank on which anything could be written.

In one corner sat a banker, who now apologized to his wife for his neglect and criticism. She, knowing the many lives he had ruined, forgave him. An aging professor felt regret for the students he had seduced, and resolved to change his ways. A sailor, thinking the club a place to get a prostitute drunk, silently passed over his pay packet. Perhaps this same sad woman used the money to return to her parents' home in Düsseldorf, to introduce them to the grand-daughter they had never seen.

So it was throughout the club. Love was induced, rekindled. Regrets were abolished. Forgiveness reigned. The everyday cares, the false promises of the economic miracle, were forgotten, at least for an evening. In the cellar of the Engel, each understood the desires and hopes of the other as in the early days of courtship. They felt again their lover's uncertainties—their fear of possession, abandonment, indifference—and made an effort to assuage them.

Then the patrons filed out, up the stairs, and back into the world. Many tried to return to the club, for the effects of the drug only lasted a few hours, but the cellar would be empty. With time they would learn that the Engel moved regularly to avoid harassment from the SA and the police, who forgave nothing. Perhaps in a few days, a week, word would spread that the Engel was returning that night to Neukolln, Pankow, Tempelhof. And that night, in the warehouse district or outside an abandoned building, you would see them, a faceless queue of people stamping their feet as they waited for an unmarked door to be unlocked. On one or two occasions the crowd forced the door, squatting for hours on dirty crates, shivering, without food or drink, kicking at the rats that scuttled along the floor. Grim vigil, the coldness of uncertainty. But they could not leave, for if the latest rumour were true, if it were not a cruel confidence trick, at eleven o'clock Herr Acheson would appear with the little blue pills that made you feel something, perhaps love.

Acheson and Strasser cross a wide field, climb a hill, take a narrow path through the trees ringing the mountain. The camerawork is unsteady, dipping and rising with the terrain. The shot is low-angle as Acheson describes the music at Bayreuth. Strasser, toting the heavy camera, tires, starts to lag behind. As the old man talks about the Engel years, the light is shaded by trees. At one point Strasser trips over some underbrush. He stumbles, almost falls.

Acheson takes the lead as they navigate the path, and so the shot is from the rear, in silhouette. He's miming now, the professor enjoying the blind meanderings his story is taking. He bends forward as if greeting an Engel customer, he passes out pills to a shrub, a tree, spine Prussian-stiff as he bows to the past, to the skyline beyond the woods.

"It was very moving, those evenings at the Engel," Acheson says distantly, the light *kavod*, the glory of the past. "It gave me a vision. It helped me understand love."

Strasser turns for the point-of-view shot: grey smoke, crooked streets, din of traffic. From this vantage everything is distant and may be beautiful.

TWO

Everything can be tested, altered. Yes, even love. Acheson tightens the sash of his silk dressing gown and settles down to read on the window seat overlooking the dark rain of Montreal. There is a paper on the neurochemistry of love, newly published, that he has meant to read. Interesting that the early phases of infatuation do not differ biologically from the obsessions of the mentally ill.

It has taken fifty years to validate his theories. The next step would, of course, be to induce the effect. Every event must be reproducible. There would be no lack of volunteers. For who would not wish to fall in love?

She arrived at his office in tears and thanked him for agreeing to see her on such short notice.

"Doctor," she said, "I am desperate and it is difficult to get away. You understand…?"

She had been told about the Engel. During one of those interminable weekends, a family friend, Putzi, had mentioned the club. He was always with them at their mountain retreat; he was so amusing and played the piano to keep everyone entertained. Even her uncle…

"Do you know my uncle, Doctor?"

"I have not had the pleasure."

"If you wish, I can arrange it."

Acheson let the matter drop. He did not wish to discuss her uncle; it was not always wise to draw too near the chancellor. Several of his acquaintances had dropped out of sight. There was much talk, rumours. The actress, Fraulein Renata, had insinuated to Acheson that the man's impulses were abnormal; he enjoyed being kicked by her like a dog. The scandal sheets had insinuated that several highly placed members of the Party were homosexuals; some wondered what this said about Hitler himself.

"My uncle…" Geli did not know how to continue. She was unaccustomed to such talk; in another time surely her destiny would have been to spend her life in the outside air, hiking the mountains, plunging into a glacier lake far away from those who would watch her innocently disrobe. The sufferings of *la jeune fille austrienne*, so healthy and blonde, so unlike the dark, sallow complexion of her uncle.

"I understand," Acheson said. "Please go on." It surprised him little that Hitler would find this young Brunhild so attractive.

"He has shown me certain attentions. His eyes follow me everywhere. He tries to draw close. I do not know how to respond. I have broached the subject with my mother, but she does not wish to discuss it. She says he is a very great man. The others—those men he surrounds himself with—are envious. I can feel it. They admire and love him—that is the only way I can explain it. I do not. Not in that way."

"But you wish to?"

She is uncertain. She cannot leave her uncle and wants the doctor to prescribe something that will make his company more bearable. In truth she is in love with someone else, a chauffeur. When her uncle discovered the affair, he was furious. He forbade her to see Emil alone. Now if she is to see him her uncle insists on accompanying them. He goes for long drives with them in the country while his officials remain at the house waiting to discuss important matters. All she wants is Emil, to be alone with him. Her uncle knows this but kisses and pets her in the back of the car, all the time studying the expression on the chauffeur's face, enjoying their suffering. The situation has grown intolerable. She cannot go on. If only she could arouse certain feelings for her uncle, it would be so much easier. She has felt so desperate, unsure where to turn. Until Putzi mentioned…

Acheson prescribed a conservative dose, fifty milligrams. Geli— Fraulein Raubal—returned to Munich and the apartments on the Prinz-Regentenstrasse she shared with her uncle. Acheson never saw her again.

He continued to follow the case over the years, of course, the few details he could glean from the reactionary press, police reports he obtained from a friend in Bavaria whose name he can no longer remember.

He wanted her to sing. Perhaps something from Wagner. No? Then a popular song, "Falling in Love Again"? She was not as beautiful as Dietrich to be sure, but she had other qualities, a reserve the actress lacked as she removed her stockings. He enjoyed seeing her hands tremble, the perspiration on her upper lip as she unbuttoned her blouse.

He lay back on the floor as he had lain on the field at Ypres. She was his Moon Child, standing before him nude, hands fluttering nervously below her belly, waiting. "You are very beautiful." Her hidden blondness was a Sera sun, a source of light and wisdom that he basked in.

At Ypres in the cannonade fire he could feel the progress of the war, had foretold years before that the Kaiser would lose. The earth heaved; it was as if the sky had split and in the unknowable darkness that lay beyond he felt the embrace of destiny. He could feel its warmth on his face like liquid sunshine, taste the acrid yellow on his lips, the Viking purity in his mouth. As the gas rolled up the hill at Werwick, he did not flinch, did not close his eyes even as they itched and burned. Would not look away but stared directly into the urine stream as Geli stood over him. He opened his mouth, tongue teasing his moustache, the pearls of gold falling like mustard tears.

Geli's psychology is unknowable to Acheson even now. She remained in the apartments with her uncle, exchanged notes, saw him when he wasn't running hither and yon about the country, still the *Meldegänger*. That summer they vacationed in the Obersalzburg. There was no hint of disagreement. She swam in the lake, water cooling the blood to ease her headaches, the coagulopathy that turned her urine red. If she was unhappy, perhaps there was not sufficient drug; he had only given her a few months' supply. He could not be held responsible if she did not comply.

No one could have known what would follow. At the end of that summer Geli ended her life. Like the actress Renata Muller, another of Hitler's conquests. Like Eva Braun herself. Geli took her uncle's pistol and shot herself in the left breast, again like Eva. In that bunker had Eva's death been a restaging of Geli's suicide? Also unknowable.

Light patter of rain on leaded glass, rain on the pavement and streets, collecting in the sewers, running down to the river. Yellow rain like old tears brushed away, best forgotten.

THREE

It was early spring when Shawnadithit led her mother and sister through the snows of the interior toward the coast. They could no longer survive alone and could only go to the settlement to beg for mercy, if it could be found there. By the bank of a river, they came upon a trapper, an ugly man with large warts and a fiery red beard. The trapper levelled his musket at them. The women sank to their knees in the snow. No one spoke, nothing broke the silence. For what word, sacred or profane, can deflect fate? At such moments there is no worthwhile thought, nothing to consider. Prayer only fills the air like static until the matter has been decided. Death is deaf, sightless. It gropes blindly, striking a stranger as it stumbles by.

The trapper, known as Cull, grabbed Shawnadithit by the arm and forced her to her feet. He gestured that she and the others should follow him. There was no mercy in his face. Shawnadithit did not understand why their lives were spared, knew nothing of the

£100 bounty on their heads. And yet they followed him, a forced march east along the riverbank.

They had not travelled far when they heard a shout. Out of a stand of pines a Beothuk appeared, a tall, painfully thin man in torn deerskins. He was running in terror from another trapper who was hunting him. Shawnadithit cried out: the man was her father, who had become separated from them during the winter and had been presumed dead.

Her father froze as he saw Cull aiming his musket. The second trapper was almost upon him. In panic he turned to the river, running onto the spring ice as if it were a bridge. Then the ice gave way and he was gone.

Cull crawled across the ice on his belly, peering through the hole at the rushing water. Shawnadithit's father did not reappear.

Ondine lies motionless in the bath, water flat, stagnant. A private moment to scry, not the brand of water divination that Mannekin recommends. Of course, he's visually adept; he can see pictures flicker in his crystal ball, like documentary stills.

But in the high wattage of the bathroom Ondine sees only an underwater magnification, pores a moonscape, a pubic rat's nest. Her body is autopsy: an angry pimple, an old scar on her knee, a yellow-green bruise on her shin from the attack at the shopping centre. Artifacts, the body's history that only the body remembers. Skin is fragile, easily damaged, punctured. A body can disappear as swift as sleight of hand, a Mannekin act. Immersed in water it is a miracle the body doesn't dissolve. Who said that? Picasso? She is too tired to think. The shopping centre, the dream: it has been a long week.

Ondine tries napping but dreams of Shawnadithit's capture, the keen of the seabirds as the three women were loaded onto a boat, the ringing of a bell as they sailed into port. She awakens, tears stinging her cheeks like a salt wind.

The telephone is ringing. It's Strasser. "I was thinking about our conversation. I'm in the middle of something right now, but I was hoping we could get together later."

She doesn't pretend to recognize the voice.

"We met yesterday. Robert Strasser."

"Who?"

She isn't sure if she wants to see Strasser again. She is in no mood to be interviewed. Or is it a date? Should she cancel? She touches the water as if it were Ouija: yes, no? She is too tired to answer questions. He will express interest, try to draw her out, but she will know he is probing, trying to uncover something. She already senses his impatience. When she was trying to explain things to him at the coffee shop, she could see he wasn't really listening. He was news-gathering. He was thinking about his next question. An occupational hazard? While he's recording he doesn't have to think; his reaction to her words would come later, when he was in the editing room, alone with her image. When she can no longer respond to him. When she is case history.

Ondine appears calm when Strasser arrives. She leads him into the living room, tells him to sit. She gestures vaguely toward a couch and armchair as if they are found objects. Her voice is casual: "Sit anywhere you like."

Strasser paces to the window, looks out, as if he can only stay a moment. She remains near the door, her eyes following him warily. Strasser smiles, but that seems to make the tension worse. He spots a couple of cats chasing dust balls under the furniture. "Cute," he says. "What are their names?"

Ondine hesitates, stuck for an answer. "They came with the apartment," she says finally. Her eyes flicker over to the kitchen as if her mind were fleeing the room. "Drink?"

"Whatever you're having."

"I can't mix my meds."

"Right."

She gets him a gin and tonic and they sit on her balcony overlooking the alley. Strasser starts to ask a question, but a garbage truck—rumbling, hydraulics, the clatter of cans—drowns out his voice. He remains silent after the truck goes, unsure of where to lead the conversation. "I don't know much about you."

"Do you about anyone?"

"I like to think so."

"I'm sure you do."

The conversation falters, trips, strays off and is lost. Like his interview with Acheson today, which makes Strasser tired just thinking about it. He doesn't have the energy to probe, put the anecdotes into context, follow the hypertextual ramblings. The effort won't lead him to truth; he's beginning to sense that now. Or worse: there may not be enough he can use.

"I saw the old man today. He told me he had a club in Berlin. Sounded like a front. He said he developed a pill that made people fall in love. Basically he was dealing."

"Is that going to be in your documentary?"

Strasser isn't sure. "It may not be true. He might have been fucking with me. Some people get off on that—bullshitting the media."

"How can you do a documentary if you don't believe the people you're interviewing?"

"That's the trick."

"Maybe he was trying to tell you something important."

"It's bullshit."

"Is it?"

"Isn't it?"

Ondine takes Strasser to a club off la Gauchetière near Chinatown. There is no sign. She takes his hand and leads him down a small flight of steps.

It is an abandoned sweatshop. Strasser can see ghostly figures in blacklight, *revenants* moving in slow motion across the dance floor. The lighting is eerie, retro. White objects in the room—a poster for a subarctic beer, a blouse, the stripes from a Dr. Seuss outfit—fluoresce and shimmer like cobalt. The room is radioactive. Ondine's face is purple, a drug side effect. Strasser starts to pull back.

"It's all right," Ondine tells him. "They know me here." To Strasser it sounds like, "Anomie here," but that doesn't make any sense. The technobeat is a tremor on his paranoia button. The bass line feels like cardiac arrest.

They find a table near the bar under a Jimi Hendrix poster. Black art deco. At the bar a vile child is rubbing an anesthetic gel on her gums. It isn't Strasser's scene, but he doesn't want to complain to Ondine. At least not yet, not this soon.

The anesthete appears at the table, does a perfect imitation of a waitress. "The usual?"

Ondine nods, including Strasser in the gesture. "Is that all right?"

"You know her?"

"I told you. I used to come here a lot. Before."

"And now?"

"Not so much."

The music is loud, and Strasser waits for the song to end. It never does. The speakers pound out endless variations of the same rhythm. Couples, groups, drift onto the dance floor then, as if hearing something—a carrier wave, a shift in the ultrasonics—they drift off again. To Strasser there is no discernible change. The music continues.

The crowd is young—teens, early twenties—and dressed like a casting call: evening gown and tux, togas and tiaras, suits and slouch hats. Movies, Strasser realizes, they're dressed like Rick and Ilsa, Clark and Carole, Nick and Nora. Images of style or faded romance.

When the drinks come, they are an amino-acid slurry. Strasser grimaces at the taste. "Is this what people drink?"

"You don't like it here," Ondine says, not a question really, her voice flat as forensics. A deep worry line appears between her eyes. "Do you hate the music?"

Strasser smiles mildly. "I prefer songs with lyrics."

"Why?" Ondine asks him, genuinely confused. "Why do you

want to listen to someone else's story? All you need is the rhythm. This band's perfect for that, all borderline types."

"I didn't realize the music was live."

"You didn't think it was music, more like some kind of disturbance they're picking up from deep space."

Strasser smiles and orders another round, only Ondine switches to clonazepam and Coke. He notes that the club's stage is empty, thinks maybe she's putting one over on him.

"Trust me," Ondine says. "The band plays behind a curtain. Some kind of purist thing. Don't want anything to distract from the music."

"Are you sure it's them playing?"

"You have to believe."

"Maybe some night they'll pull back the curtain and there'll be nothing there."

"You gotta have faith."

"You expect me to buy that?"

"I thought you would," Ondine says. "It's a lyric." It's a point in her favour, but Ondine doesn't seem to be keeping score. "You like to believe that you don't believe in anything."

"Is that what you think?"

"I think that's why you're alone."

"Acheson told me people aren't a jigsaw puzzle you can piece together."

"Or are you afraid that when people have put together your puzzle they'll see there's nothing there? Like those musicians," she adds, a little world-weary. "The band came to Montreal to hang out, worked the métro for a while, but there was no money in it. They saw a sign at the psych department, some experiment gig: LOOKING FOR HUMAN GUINEA PIGS. MUST BE WILLING TO SIGN A CONSENT FORM. They got paid thirty bucks to lie in the dark in a tank of water."

Strasser's done a piece on that very thing. "Sensory deprivation. You float in a tank of salt water that's heated to body temperature."

"Like watching TV in the bathtub. Only without a TV people start to hallucinate. There's nothing for your mind to fix on so it creates its own images. The mind can't tolerate a blank screen. It's why we dream. It's why you got your own show. We need the pictures so we can hold on to reality, otherwise everything starts to slip."

Soft bodies animated by the soft crystal glow of the TV screen, ten o'clock and consciousness is starting to slip. "Good evening, tonight on *Notable Lives…*"

"So the band," Strasser asks, "what did they see—cartoons, the face of God?"

"Nothing."

"You can't look inside your mind and see nothing there."

"Call it an anomaly. They got in the tank and nothing happened. A couple of hours passed and no hallucinations. They just shut down. Then it got weird. A lab assistant was keeping an eye on them. He went out for coffee and got into a car accident. Went to the hospital and everybody forgot all about the experiment. Then it was the weekend. On Monday one of the researchers saw they were still in the tank and hauled them out. The docs freaked—some kind of ethical violation, afraid they were going to blow their research grant. They checked them out, asked, 'Are you okay?' And they were like, 'Yeah, whatever.' They were in there for three days and they were thinking *bonus*. 'We're going to make, like, more money.'" Ondine smiles. "Ninety bucks, but somebody had to tell them. They couldn't do the math."

So the four lads passed days in a deep blue sea, didn't even have to stir themselves to take a leak, fluids ebbing and flowing, couldn't really tell if that warm stuff they were floating in was heavy-duty salination or piss, not that it mattered. So maybe after a few days the mind had a tendency to drift to the fringe—the occult, UFOs, Elvis sightings—but that only helped their move into the marketplace.

Of course, there was a follow-up, the scientists now sticking to the research protocol as if it were a holy formula. The band showed no ill effects, demonstrated age-appropriate behaviour for their cohort. "They ended up publishing a paper," Ondine says. "'Autism as a Form of Ego Preservation in the Media Age'—something like that. A record company exec picks up on it and sees an angle he can work.

Gives them a new name, comes up with a Night of the Living Braindead image, something bogus, so they ditched the company and play here."

"Why'd they volunteer to be lab rats?"

The question doesn't interest Ondine. "Maybe they needed the money. Maybe they just didn't give a shit."

"Why'd you used to come here?"

She shrugs. "I thought maybe the music would get in my head, do something."

"Like what?"

"Rewire it."

"And then what?"

"Something will change."

"Something?"

She looks at him almost apologetically. "Me."

Strasser lets the comment go untouched, like his drink. She watches him scanning the room for their waitress, sees he's having a hard time, and slides his drink toward him. "Do it," she says urgently. "You think it's easy for me to come here? This is ground zero. If the sky falls, it's going to be here. I'm trying to help you."

Strasser gingerly sips his drink, winces at the taste, like rat shit. "You're saying you want me to change?"

"You don't understand," Ondine says with surprising ferocity. "You don't get what all this is about. Drugs, music, new relationships, new environments—don't you see? We want change. We're trying to affect things. Make ourselves into something different. We don't like the way it is. We don't like who we are."

Strasser sets down his drink. "You sound like Acheson."

"That's just one way, diagnostic Tao, whatever. There are other paths. Holism, healing, esoterica, meditation." Strasser looks skeptical, and Ondine backs off. "Bullshit, right? That's what you say."

"What do you say?"

"What *they* say—change the system from within."

"I don't think that's what *they* meant."

"The only way things are going to change is if we change ourselves."

Strasser feels himself getting irritated. "One brain cell at a time?"

"If that's what it takes."

"You don't fuck with the mind."

"You do."

"This isn't about me."

"Audience surveys, demographic breakdowns, they're just a feedback loop, a circle jerk. Then you just try to push the right buttons to get a response."

"If there's no response, it means you haven't communicated."

"Every stimulus doesn't induce communication. Sometimes it's just annoying."

"You're thinking *Notable Lives*?"

"You don't know what I'm thinking."

No, Strasser figures, and orders a drink. She's trying to provoke him, prod him into a response. But that's his job. He's the one trying to get her to say something for the camera. "We're working the same side of the street," he says after the waitress brings another round. "We're both trying to put together the bits and pieces of a person's life." Strasser the bridge builder. "You with that Native woman, me with Acheson."

"I'm trying to understand her, to know how she felt."

"Don't you think I'm trying to do the same?"

"How? All you're thinking about is beginning, middle, end. Acheson: The Early Years. Acheson: The Years of Struggle. It's linear, Strasser. It's boring."

Strasser flushes. "What would you have me do?"

"Do you think any of it means anything? It isn't about events—not with those people, maybe not with anyone. It's about having this idea, how it fucks everyone up."

"You sound like Acheson again," Strasser mutters before he loses audio, trying not to think about work. But he's running the Acheson tapes in his mind like a demo reel, the old man mouthing the words in slo-mo: *You must begin with an idea...*

Strasser's ready to bail out on the project, scrounge up another subject, only it's no good. Even now he can hear the old man's voice coming back to him unbidden, freak signal, lost soul in a maelstrom of atmospheric disturbance. *What is it you wish from me?*

He is surprised to see Ondine crying. "You're just fucking around," she says. "You're not serious. It's about control, Strasser. It's about all the shit they try to cram into our heads, all the rules. It's all one big fucking experiment. They're trying to make us—you, me, all the fucked-up people in here—*into* something. Social animals, good citizens, whatever. So they dick around. It's supposed to work, but it never does, not really. They can't control the variables, the environment, the way people are. So it goes out of control. It gets out. It goes wild. And people get hurt."

FOUR

In the summer of 1952 a woman of twenty-three, Mary P., was referred to the Institute for treatment of a nervous complaint. She reported a loss of appetite, poor sleep, jumpiness, and feelings of tension that would not go away. There was no prior history of mental disturbance.

Mary was the eldest daughter of seven children. Her parents had died when she was sixteen, and she had taken a job in a large downtown department store to support the family. She had performed well and had been promoted to a senior sales position. Two years prior to presentation Mary had married James P., a buyer at the store. The couple took an apartment in the downtown area and were saving to buy a house. Mary was extremely meticulous and kept a careful account of their finances, enabling her to provide some support to her siblings. She was very devout.

At the first meeting her husband reported that Mary took on the sins of the world and worried too much about her family and money matters. Her only hobby was housecleaning, which she performed with dedication and great attention. Mary herself admitted to a fixity of mind with respect to cleanliness, which she ascribed to the influence of her father. The latter had been stricken during the influenza pandemic after the Great War and had become obsessed with germs and contamination. Complications of influenza had left the father in a weakened condition, contributing to a sporadic employment history and alcoholism.

The patient reported that following her marriage she had become increasingly tense and distraught, with periods of amenorrhea. Her doctor had prescribed rest, and Mary and her husband had taken an extended vacation in upstate New York. This period of calm did not alleviate her nervousness. She was unable to concentrate and worried about losing her job, which would prevent her from buying a house and starting a family. She told her husband her periods of gloom were penance for sins she had committed. In private consultation Mary confessed she was afraid her husband would tire of her frequent complaints, abandon her, leaving her destitute. She felt she was losing her soul.

The physical examination was unremarkable. The patient was a twenty-three-year-old nulliparous female, one hundred twenty-five pounds, with even features, mid-length black hair in the current style, and green eyes. She was, in a haunted sort of way, quite beautiful.

As Strasser is loading his equipment into the van, he is summoned to Dr. Baum's office by an Institute guard.

"You have been consuming a significant amount of Dr. Acheson's time," the research director notes. "Do you mind my asking what you've been discussing?"

"His research. He mentioned an early breakthrough. A new drug he developed. He said his father gave him the idea."

"Dr. Acheson didn't develop the chemical," Baum interrupts. "I believe it was synthesized at Merck. Perhaps it is a small point. But if these interviews are to proceed they must adhere to the facts. I'm afraid I must insist on this. There is no place for anecdotal evidence." He smiles like a man who doesn't acknowledge anger. "What did Dr. Acheson say about this drug?"

Strasser wishes he had the tape handy to cue his memory. He doesn't remember Acheson's exact words. All he has are visual impressions, images. "He mentioned a club. The Engel. It was during the Depression. That was where they used the drug."

"A sort of group therapy?"

"I suppose."

"Did he mention where this club was located?"

"No." Strasser corrects himself. "Yes, it moved all the time. It didn't have a permanent location."

"So it cannot be traced? There won't be any photographs of it, something to use in your documentary?"

"I have the interview, what Dr. Acheson remembers."

"I see." The doctor runs his fingers through the sparse cornrows of hair on his forehead, fingering the hair plugs as if trying to read their thoughts. "It seems to me that these interviews with Dr. Acheson won't really capture the story. People are unreliable. False memory syndrome and all that. I'm sure you would like hard information. But all you seem to have, frankly, is gossip. This story about a club of drug addicts—it tends to give the wrong impression. You understand my point."

"Was this drug some sort of secret?"

"There are no secrets in science," Baum says officiously. "We're rather like television that way. Everything's out in the open."

"Maybe you can give some more details to flesh out the story."

The doctor hesitates, frozen in a kind of inner debate.

"The camera's outside," Strasser says helpfully. "It'll be off the record."

"What do you want to know?"

"Just a bit of background history."

"As far as history is concerned, the drug was a curiosity, an anomaly," Baum begins. "Not every idea is viable, you understand. There is a natural selection. Bad ideas are weeded out and forgotten. History is quite right to be merciless in that regard." He leans back in his chair. "It was a long time ago. Scientists back then used to develop chemicals that had no particular purpose. Absurd really. They put together compounds like Tinkertoys. Curiosity, I suppose. I'm not criticizing. If people weren't curious, there wouldn't be any science to discuss. The Merck chemists developed a number of amphetamine derivatives. They had the usual stimulatory properties. It was only later that a few people—Dr. Acheson among them—found that these drugs enhanced certain mood states. They called the drugs empathogens."

"As in empathy?" Strasser asks. "Love?"

"Only a chemist would call it love. I'm sure you have more romantic notions."

"Did these drugs work?"

"That's not really the question. There was no market for them. This was just before the war—the Nazis, Churchill, all that. Not love's finest hour." He smiles at his witticism. "Before your time, at any rate."

"So you're saying the research was abandoned?"

"Yes."

"Nothing more was done?"

"I would know," Baum says unequivocally. "I'm in charge of new chemical entities." That same smile. "I'll admit we did play about with it for a few years. There was a bit of a revival in the sixties, a time when even the shabbiest notions got aired out and recycled. The analysts thought the drug would help them break down their patients' emotional resistance."

"You never used it?"

"I'd made the move to research by then. I stopped seeing patients. It was more interesting to develop new compounds."

"Ones with more market potential?"

"I'd prefer to think of them as better ideas. Empathogens have no place in our present research, something Dr. Acheson might have mentioned to you." He shrugs apologetically. "I'm afraid he has not remained up-to-date with our current activities. The mind grows tired. The past has greater appeal. You can understand that Dr. Acheson has a certain nostalgia for his early days in Berlin."

"You mean the Engel club?"

"That's just something he imagined. In English *Der Engel* means the Angel. It was an idea left over from the first war. The soldiers used to imagine an angel flying over the trenches. Angel of Mercy. Or Death." He shrugs "Either way. It was amphetamine psychosis. Drugs were part of the ration in those days, a means of fighting fatigue. They didn't concern themselves with the psychiatric effects. It was quite mad obviously. I suppose the men felt an angel was going to swoop down and save them from the war. In time the story made the rounds, something that got trotted out when a few of the lads got together at one of the beer halls. I'm sure there was a bit of the old-time religion tossed in, no atheists in foxholes. It was something to believe in. But it wasn't anything real. Of course, that's never the point, is it? It doesn't have to be real for people to believe in it. For a scientist it's another matter entirely. We realized that the phenomenon was a remnant, a bit of displaced memory, a metaphor, if you will. That's all. I'm sure that's what Dr. Acheson meant. He wanted to give your documentary a bit of flavour. He was just ladling out a taste of nostalgia."

FIVE

It was a sickness: nostalgia. A neuralgia of the mind. An ache for the past, for what had been. For home. There was a sense of bewilderment, with circumstances, with who we have become. It is uncertain when it begins. The symptoms: fatigue, loss of concentration, irritability, feelings of hopelessness, memories. It was a subtype of depression, a dysthymia of the soul.

The prognosis was poor. The condition was often fatal. During the Second World War, on the drive to the east, the deaths numbered in the thousands. As winter set in, the men lost hope that they would ever see home again. In the trenches around Stalingrad, in the blinding static of snow, they saw a vision of Heimweh. The myth took many forms, as with all myths. She was Valerian to the Russians; to the English, Amphetamina. To some the Angel of the battlefield was Ialdebaoth, the demiurge blinded by snow. Or Samael, consort of Lilith, who brought knowledge of the horror. As the Angel's wings hissed overhead, the soldiers dropped their weapons and lay down uncovered in the heart of snow, numb in the Arctic cold.

Dr. Baum felt that cold in the winter of 1952. He had been given the assignment of investigating new chemical compounds believed to exist in subarctic vegetation. It was Dr. Acheson's idea to send him to Yellowknife. It meant several months in the field, but Baum had been told by Dr. Acheson personally that he would be awarded a new appointment on his return.

He couldn't refuse. Dr. Acheson was already something of a legend. He had pioneered much of the early work on brain chemicals. His papers on psychoactive substances were required reading by the faculty. His lectures were aggressively modern. The residents naturally held him in awe. Dr. Acheson stories regularly made the rounds: he had consulted with Freud, was the original Dr. Mabuse, had slept with the actress Pola Negri. There was even one apocryphal tale about his fateful flight from Germany near the end of the war. Acheson on his escape to Switzerland had masqueraded as the B-girl Lola-Lola. They were near the border when the doctor's musky perfume attracted the attentions of a junior officer in the Abwehr, who insisted on a hand job before allowing Lola-Acheson to cross the frontier. In the end he got away, of course. Acheson always blessed with the touch of an artist.

Baum accepted the Yellowknife assignment. He was permitted one question. "Why the north?"

"The vegetation is unique," Dr. Acheson told him. "Cocaine, nicotine, alkaloids—these are known. But what is known about the subarctic? Nothing. Go there. Talk to the people. Make a discovery."

"We could synthesize new chemicals in the lab."

"A waste of time," Acheson said dismissively. "The research, the trial and error, is done. Nature is a laboratory, Baum. God is a chemist. Force Him to tell you His secrets."

He spent the long winter in a cabin beside a lake. He set up a small laboratory. His equipment was crude, the tests rudimentary. He only had to identify a half-dozen compounds that could be investigated further on his return. That would be enough. They would complete the more complex analyses in Montreal. Baum would receive his promotion. He would be assigned a small research team.

The experiments failed. In the field samples he obtained he found little of interest.

In the mail bag that spring were a dozen letters requesting information on his progress. The last letter was two months old. After that, nothing. He could feel himself being forgotten.

He enlisted the help of Lily, a Dogrib woman who eked out a living trading to the radium miners. She cooked for him, cleaned the cabin. He wanted her to sleep with him during that long, long winter, but she rejected him. She withdrew to the town, and he didn't see her again until the spring. He hoped that if he hired her, paid her money to help him collect and classify the varieties of vegetation… But she didn't understand Baum's fascination with plants.

"They are to eat?" she asked.

"No."

"But you cook them." She had watched him perform experiments in his makeshift lab.

"I make medicines."

This she understood. He was a shaman, *angakut*, but a poor one. Not like Anaqpiaq. He was the greatest shaman.

Baum saw an opportunity. "I wish to become a great shaman. Can you take me to see this man, Anaqpiaq?"

Lily refused. Anaqpiaq did not like white men. Baum persisted. The local medicine man could save Baum some time. It seemed the utmost priority to wrap up his experiments as soon as possible and return to civilization.

"You will take me, yes?" He didn't try to hide his desperation. He didn't give a damn what she would charge him. She could have his equipment, his supplies, all of it. "Tomorrow?"

"Rain will come," she said.

Baum shook his head forcefully. "Tomorrow."

They headed into the bush at dawn, walking all day in the rain until Baum was footsore, ready to drop from exhaustion. The trail was unmarked, and they seemed to have wandered far north of the

DEW line. Baum fell often. He asked Lily to stop, to take a break. He needed a rest. He needed a cigarette. He cried with fatigue. He grew angry and shouted at her, but she never looked back. She pressed on, and Baum had to struggle after her. He was afraid that if he lost sight of her he would never find his way home. He was afraid to be left alone.

It was late in the evening when they heard voices. After Lily's silence, Baum found that the sound made him strangely anxious. He called out to Lily, but she had disappeared. He felt himself beginning to panic and started running through the thick brush, fireweed tangling his feet, thorns tearing at his arms.

Then he was clear. In the distance a group of Natives huddled around a small fire. Lily turned as Baum stumbled toward them. "*Angakut*," she said, gesturing at an old man dressed in ritual robes of catskin. "Shaman."

Baum collapsed in the dirt. He felt as if he were about to weep with fatigue. "Great shaman, I have come many miles to find you. I desire to see." It was a ritual, something he had read in a book Dr. Acheson had given him, a formula. There was always a formula.

The old man grunted and motioned for Baum to sit beside him. A woman stepped out of the darkness, offering a stone bowl filled with a dark liquid. Baum took a small sip. It tasted like mown grass and rat shit.

The old man began to sing. Baum couldn't understand the words, but the tune was familiar, something that was always playing on the radio.

> Good night, Irene
> Good night, Irene
> I'll see you in my dreams…

Baum felt overwhelmed with fatigue. His thoughts were dull, woolly, as if he had been drugged. He felt sleepy. The men continued to chant. The ceremony seemed endless, repetitive, as if somewhere along the way the Natives had taken a wrong step and had gotten lost. The old woman offered him another sip from the bowl.

After an hour, the *angakut* motioned to the others to be silent. "In the beginning…" the old man said. Baum tried not to yawn. He wasn't in the mood to hear another lurid creation myth.

Only the old man's story sounded different. "I am *angakut*, the last shaman. Once there was great magic in the world. No more. After me it is finished."

It had not always been so. As Baum fought to stay awake, the old man explained that once the shaman had been a power and inspiration to his people. For joy alone he would explore the world, flying through space to the highest level or burrowing down to the underworld of evil and memory. But there was joy no more. The great mysteries were being consumed. The shaman's powers were fading; he could no longer fly great distances. Everything was past. The future was a dark night with no dawn. The old man's tale meandered into silence, his voice trailing off into melancholy.

Baum fought to stay awake. "If you could help me…" he said, his voice slurred and almost unintelligible. He was powerfully thirsty but wasn't sure if he should drink any more of the Native potion. He felt a slow retardation, as if his responses were being interrupted, delayed, as if he were winding down.

The shaman seemed to diagnose the problem and was quick to act. He reached out and grasped Baum's shoulder in a fierce grip. "Come."

The old man stood slowly, knees cracking like firewood. He gestured for Baum to follow. Baum swigged at the Native brew for courage and hurried after him into the brush. After a short walk, they came to the entrance of an abandoned mine guarded by an old dog that looked rabid.

"What is this place?"

"You come."

The *angakut* took Baum's flashlight and led him down two levels to where the air was thin and heavy with dust. On the third level Baum sank to his knees. "Help me," he cried out. He felt as if he were going to pass out.

The old man forced Baum's shoulders to the ground, pinched off his nose, and breathed lustily into his mouth. "We go to the home of Takanakapsaluk, the mother of the sea beasts."

Baum nodded weakly, sickened by the taste of tobacco juice and tooth rot from the old man's mouth.

They descended two more levels. The old man stopped. "Enter," he said, his voice as hollow as the earth. "The way is open. The way is clear!"

It sounded like more code work, something Acheson's book hadn't mentioned. Three men stepped out of the shadows and pinned Baum's arms to his sides. They pulled him along the tunnel and down a small shaft. Baum tried to shout out, but there wasn't enough air to carry his cries. The three men tied him to a crossbeam and started to cut away his clothes with long knives until he was stripped bare in the thin light.

"What do you want?" Baum asked.

His voice was drowned out by the men ululating. *Halalala-hehehe*. The noise was deafening. More terrifying was the silence that followed. At the far end of the darkness Baum heard a shuffling of bare feet. The old man stepped out of the shadows, naked and wrinkled like a formalin brain. Baum tried to look away, but the men roughly bound his head to a support beam with a leather belt.

The shaman held up a long whalebone instrument attached to an animal bladder. "Shit chaser," he whispered. "I give to Josefstalin. I give to you. White men full of shit."

Baum began to cry as the old man administered the enema. They excoriated him with wild grasses, flayed his skin with strips of caribou hide.

After a time they seemed to grow tired of the rituals. The men withdrew into the tunnel. Baum was left alone. The cavern was damp, and Baum couldn't stop shivering. The only sounds he could make out were the rats scuttling along the walls, their shrieks in the darkness feeling like claws tearing along his spine. He listened to their falsetto screams for hours, a day, two. On the third day the rats attacked, attracted by the smell of fear and excrement. They bit his legs. He kicked at them and they retreated for a time, but he could see their red eyes watching him. They were regrouping, plotting strategy. A day later they attacked again.

SIX

In late spring of 1823, Shawnadithit, her mother, and her sister were taken two hundred miles by small boat to St. John's. At Government House the women were provided with beds, which they did not use. The sister was ill, and a military surgeon attended the young woman. He recommended opening a vein, but the sight of the lancet terrified the girl and he was unable to perform the procedure. The women were given English clothing and were taken shopping, which caused much disturbance among the citizenry.

Unsure what to do with the three Beothuks, the government released the women a few days later. They were taken to the Bay of Exploits, then upriver to the site of an abandoned Native village. They were provided with a small supply of food but no shelter. Unable to hunt for food and with her sister dying of tuberculosis, Shawnadithit half carried, half dragged her sister back to a fishing station on the coast to beg for help. A fisherman allowed the women to stay in a lean-to on the shore where Shawnadithit's sister expired soon afterward. A week later her mother also died.

Now alone, Shawnadithit paddled across the bay to the residence of John Peyton, the local magistrate. She was taken into the household and allowed to wash floors, lay the fire, do the laundry, and make tea for the magistrate. She acted well and was considered a willing and industrious servant.

If Shawnadithit was traumatized by recent events, it went unrecorded. She was reportedly happy and willingly joined in the activities of the Peyton household. But she slept badly and had visions of the *mudeet*, the bad man who had come to kill her.

⊕

Ondine studies herself in the mirror, tries to imagine the *mudeet*. She wonders if the word was a corrupted variation of *maudit*. Damned. The early missionaries, when they first came upon the heathens, had asked the question: *Est-ce qu'ils sont maudits?* Are they damned? The question itself, in the static of time, would come to define the Natives: *les esquimaux*. Wild creatures, soulless as golems.

Ondine looks at her face's reflection, wonders what is going on inside. Or is it just skeleton, bone? Applies a little blush called Passion Petechia, highlighting the cheekbones to make them sharp. Counts the lines now appearing, Ondine feeling like an old soul forced to renew her lease on earth till the end of the world because of some past misdeeds, in every wrinkle lay a sorrow generations old. Digs into her makeup bag and applies more colour to her forehead, along the jawline, across the breastbone. Steps back from the mirror and lets the deerskin dress fall to the floor. She traces her nipples in burgundy lipstick and outlines her ribs, hipbones, the line of her thighs. In the forest-green of the bathroom she sees a pine landscape reflected on the water. Through a spyglass someone is watching from a ship offshore. The red makeup is a warning. Are the men watching her afraid? Will they think twice before they venture to this newfound land where the women paint their skins the colour of blood?

⊕

The *mudeet* was a local Micmac named Noel Boss, a hunter who frequently visited the Peytons and would see Shawnadithit there. Noel liked to boast that he had killed ninety-nine Beothuks, only one shy of a hundred. Shawnadithit felt Noel watching her through the kitchen door as she scrubbed pots. Later she would find small drawings of killed animals—a squirrel, a rabbit—on the rear stoop, pictographs whose meaning she could not decipher. But as omens the notes were clear enough: the world had become strange, she would not survive long.

Some nights she would awaken to an odour in the air—tobacco smoke, the scent of mint—and she would feel Noel's presence in the room. She believed she saw his face appear in the firefly glow. She had fear dreams that followed her through the waking hours.

She did not try to talk about her fears to the Peytons, for that was not her nature. And how to explain these things she felt? She had been taught the words for *pot* and *tea*, *yes* and *no*, but what use were these? She held no vocabulary for the end of things.

At night Shawnadithit would go by herself into the woods and along the shore, listening to her mother's voice in the sough of trees, the rhythm of speech of the ocean. She would face out to sea, eyes tightly closed, pressing a seashell to her ear as if trying to communicate with the future.

⊕

In every shell there is a satellite uplink: listen. Can you hear someone trying to speak to you? The voice is soft. Is it a lover? Or someone whispering a warning, afraid to be overhead? But, no, something has gone wrong with the electromagnetics. There is too much interference. You can only hear the empty rhythm of the ocean: lost souls, the static of extinction.

Steam kettle hiss as Ondine makes tea, watches the steam rising like woodsmoke, like early-morning mist. She imagines a late-setting moon, a Beothuk *kuis*, but she can't see it clean. It reminds her of something from Disney, a cartoon cabala from *The Sorcerer's Apprentice*. She shudders: hates rodents, even ones on celluloid.

She can no longer think. She heard once that after the knowledge boom comes the echo: the loss of knowledge, the simple act of forgetting: Languages, symbols, technologies, the day-to-day acts of doing. Mannekin has tried to tell her how it was in Shawnadithit's time, but he doesn't know; he can only speculate. Strasser didn't even try to guess. Good, she thinks, a point in his favour. She is tired of speculations.

She doesn't know yet what to think about Strasser. Beside the teapot on the kitchen counter Ondine has a runebag the way others keep garlic. From it she draws *Oss*, the messenger of news. Like a newsman, a documentary producer? Or is it *Oss* reversed: misunderstanding, failed words cluttering her life like unwashed dishes?

Before they left the club she could have told him what was in the two, maybe three drinks he had. But in their kind of conversation there is no way to tell him lightly, just in passing, that the heart is a long-buried treasure marked by *X*.

SEVEN

He watches her make tea, the way she counts to herself as she spoons out something unbagged and godawful, an herbal tisane to help him sleep but which will keep him up half the night. She curls her toes as she pours the water, feet bare on the cold lino. People fall in love when the person is preoccupied, busy, thinking about something else. When their self-awareness loses some of its grip. When their face becomes blank with concentration, then the projection begins…

"You're staring at me," Ondine says.

"Was I? I didn't mean to. I was thinking about something else."

She doesn't ask. She sets the tray down. "The gaze," she says. "It fucks people up. Sugar?"

"No."

"The fear of two eyes staring," she says as she pours the tea. "It's the most primitive fear. I don't know. I read that somewhere."

"Is that why you're not looking at me?"

"I don't want to spill."

She is more relaxed now; he hadn't realized that going to the club was a strain on her. She tells him she doesn't get out much. Strasser wants to know more about her, is content to listen to the stories we tell when it's new and we need something to say. Anecdotes overripe with meaning now used for barter. She gives him small intimacies, minor revelations for which she no longer has any use. Mostly archival footage from the seventies and eighties: grainy, out of sequence, godawkward. Bad hairstyles, ditto fashion wear. There was an angry, rebellious period when she played street drugs like roulette, but it is a time that is difficult to conjure.

"Creative pharmaceuticals," she says, "mental stimulation, pleasure, transformation. Back then it was about changing who you were. It was supposed to be evolution, but it got all fucked up. It has to happen in the right space. Half of the effect of a drug comes from the environment. Remember Tim Leary at Harvard? Playing with acid till it got out of the lab and into the world. That's when it goes bad, when you can't control the variables. We get all heavy talking about it now, but drugs're just a sign. They're nothing on their own. We're the medium, Strasser. The whole thing—the fantasy, the pharmacology—is playing out in our heads. You look at what people are taking to figure out what people need."

"What do you need?" Strasser asks. "What did you take?"

"Never the downers, the CNS depressants, the opiates. I wanted to see what I was missing. Ten, fifteen years ago it was X."

It was Adam, a record producer from the Factory label, who had first laid some X on her. He was a DJ in a cavernous dump called the Hacienda, part of the club scene Ondine had investigated on a summer trip to Manchester, England. He introduced himself "Madam I'm Adam" in that famous palindrome, only Adam was Ecstasy, X. Ondine went for the line, but it was only a segue to sex. "Pass," she said, whereupon the DJ had actually gone down on his knees begging her to fuck him right there in the sound booth, so not cool.

Ondine starting messing around with X strictly recreational, something to improve the mood. X was the pharmacokarmic wheel, circling the globe like a chemical Eros, Libido, Jung's energy of life. She needed it. Ondine had always been on the depressive side, and in that summer of X she fell in love, maybe more than once. Was it the drugs? Who cares? The feeling itself was real: transformation.

Ondine had always sensed a barrier suspended between herself and other people, an impenetrable wall that always stopped her from making contact. That summer the wall fell. She felt free. She felt like Berlin would feel. She felt fucking fantastic.

It ended soon enough. The doorman at a nearby club, the Thunderdome, was strafed in a drive-by shooting, and the Hacienda was torched soon afterward. Firefights in the MDMA turf war.

"This MDMA," Strasser asks her, "is that the empathogen Acheson was talking about?"

"Whatever," Ondine says. "There's a whole family, MDMA, MDEA. Call it Ecstasy. Call it Adam and Eve. Call it X."

Strasser can feel a pissy mood coming on. "Sounds to me like leftover free-love bullshit from the sixties. Some of that love potion number nine."

"Maybe it is. It sounds stupid now. That was then and who gives a shit about the history?"

"They gave up on that thirty years ago," Strasser says impatiently. You're telling me it's back?"

"Some people don't forget. Ideas never go away. They wait for technology. They get transformed. We're surrounded by ideas and images that are a thousand years old. The same hopes and dreams, the same stories."

"Sure," Strasser says, "s'called reruns."

She ignores him, grips his arm. "But every now and then a new idea comes along and it gets out into the world. Maybe it's stupid or dangerous, but it still gets thrown into the mix."

"Like what?" Strasser asks. He's straining now, brain starting to hurt. "Like relativity? Like Uncertainty?"

"Like killing women and children," she says quietly, "like genocide." For an instant he feels her slipping away, Strasser tracking the movement of a shadow in the trees. When she returns, her voice is a little more distant. "It wasn't like that once upon a time," she insists, sounding like a fairy tale that neither of them believes.

She keeps her hand on his arm, and Strasser is distracted by her touch, a small gesture but he can feel himself starting to respond. He tries to draw her closer. "Do you miss that feeling?"

Ondine shrugs. She can't recall. If there are memories, only the body remembers.

Strasser leans forward to kiss her, but Ondine's onto him, shuts him down. "Forget it."

"I can't." While her hand is there Strasser allows himself the vain belief that something could happen, the distance between them can be bridged. But a moment later she withdraws her hand and reaches for one of his cigarettes.

She leaves the smoke burning in the ashtray as she makes coffee. Strasser retrieves the butt, smokes it while she clatters in the kitchen, the filter touch of her lips only in his imagination.

He finishes it by the time she comes back, not paying him much attention, focusing on the tray she's carrying. Was there something, Strasser wants to know, in the chemistry, in the paraquat of chance, that led to her panic attacks?

The question is too close to the present. Ondine doesn't want to talk about it. "Don't make this into background info."

When she hands Strasser the coffee mug, he notices a thin white line on her wrist. "One of the body's memories?"

"I was in pretty bad shape for a while."

"And now?"

She doesn't answer, just shakes her head uncomfortably. She sees that the cigarette is gone and has the urge for another, but she has already smoked too much: her lungs ache, she's having trouble catching her breath, she's got emphysema. Strasser doesn't let go of her wrist. He is studying it, tracing the scar with his finger to her fate line, her heart.

"I'm sorry," he says, and brushes his lips along her palm as if a kiss will smooth the furrows, change what is written. He gently holds her chin, cradling her head as his lips move over hers. She responds tentatively, as if surprised, then kisses him feverishly, lips pressed hard against his mouth, tongue urgent. A moment later she abruptly pulls back, stares at him, the mood gone now or changed into something else. There is assessment in her eyes as if deciding, working out the angles in the geometry of nose, jaw, ear.

Under the scrutiny Strasser feels himself getting hot, flushed. "What?"

"The gaze," she says. "Now you know."

He reaches out for her, but she vanishes into the next room. Strasser expects her to return, but she doesn't. It feels absurd sitting alone in her living room, so he goes looking for her. He finds her in the bedroom by a canopy bed, nude, a candle burning as if remembering a lost soul.

Strasser crosses over to her, then hesitates. "I thought…"

"You think too much." She strips off his clothes, perfunctory like a nurse, and pulls him into her. Her nipples burn red and taste of burgundy. She grips him tight, hard, legs locked around him, arms about his neck, forehead, breasts slick with sweat. As they make love, he tries to kiss her, but she turns her face aside, her breath ragged as he presses against her, panting now in the thin, thin air.

EIGHT

C lose-up…

The examination of Mary P. revealed a slightly anorexic female, somewhat disorganized in appearance. Medical history revealed amenorrheic episodes but was otherwise not significant. On questioning the patient displayed a tendency to make self-pitying statements, engaged in hand-wringing, fidgeting, other signs of agitation. Eye contact was intermittent.

Her case would have normally been assigned to one of the residents, but Dr. Acheson intervened and conducted the initial interview personally. He rarely saw patients, and the move occasioned some comment. His interest in Mary P. was considered out of character, not pathognomonic even in that hothouse environment, but certainly noteworthy.

"You've been feeling distressed. Has anything happened recently?"

"No, nothing."

"And your marriage?"

"I don't like to say."

"You can speak freely here."

"You won't tell him?"

"These sessions are for you. What we discuss is confidential."

"I've been doing well at work. I just got a promotion."

"Did that please your husband? What was his reaction?"

"He said I wasn't spending enough time with him. I wasn't making a proper home. I know him. He wants me to get fired."

"Why would he want that?"

"He says I'm more interested in work than in him. I have to study at night if I want to get ahead. It's hard. If I lose my job, it'll be because of him. I just want us to do well."

"What does he want?"

"I don't know. He wants to start a family."

"You don't believe he has the right to want that?"

"Not now."

"You're twenty-three. When do you plan to have children?"

"I haven't thought about it. Maybe next year."

"Have you been neglecting your responsibilities at home? Your husband—"

"He's watching me."

"What gives you that impression?"

"Last week I was moving the chesterfield and found a scrap of paper. I thought we had mice. There was another piece of paper in the corner under the drapes. I knew he'd put them there."

"Did you confront him about your suspicions?"

"He brought it up. He was in a foul mood at dinner. We had a terrible row. He accused me of all sorts of things. I started to cry. It was so unfair. He dragged me into the living room. He pulled back the drapes and showed me the piece of paper. He shouted at me, 'See this!' I shouted back, 'Look at it. Look!' On the piece of paper, on every piece he'd hidden in the room, I'd written 'Ha, ha.'"

"I see. And what did this accomplish?"
"The bastard hit me."

When Orpheus descended into the Underworld to reclaim Eurydice, she was shrouded in darkness, scarcely visible to him. He saw what he had always seen, his wife unaltered by the calamities that had befallen her. But she had changed in death and had seen many things. It was there in her eyes, which the shadows kept hidden.

And as Orpheus led Eurydice back to their home, he had a moment of doubt. He looked back to see if his wife was following him. And in the half-light he saw a hardness in her face, a disapproval, in her eyes a knowledge of how things were in other places ruled by other men. She was no longer his wife. And he turned away. He let her slip back into the Underworld.

Dr. Acheson completed his notes and scheduled an interview with Mrs. P.'s husband for the next day.

Mr. P. displayed a certain suspiciousness of character when he arrived. He looked severely at the shelves of books and journals, the leather couch by the wall. "So this is where you do it." He took a seat across from the doctor, hefting aside the bronze bust of Freud so he could look directly at Acheson. "What have you got for me?"

"Your wife is very ill. She suffers from a form of conduct disorder. Such a condition often manifests in childhood as oppositional behaviour, defiance of authority, that sort of thing. She has taken a wrong path, yes? She no longer recognizes your position as the head of the household. She argues and disputes your decisions, challenges your position. Your home is a house divided. Your wife has gone astray."

"None of that was my doing."

"Our purpose is not to assess blame," Acheson assured him.

113

"We want to help your wife. The behaviours you have seen, they are only the beginning. We cannot know where her tendencies may lead. It is a question of temperament, the beliefs and attitudes she had as a child. The person you know as your wife is simply the end result of a series of decisions and actions that have led her to this point. The problem lies very deep. The troubles we see are always found in the past. So we must go back to that past and root out those behaviours that are causing her present discontent. If we can alter her, reshape the structure of her thoughts, perhaps we can lead her to a more productive life."

"Alter her?"

NINE

The mind is a city: structures, thoroughfares, parts where we conduct business, places we visit only at night. There are well-kept areas for public view, dark places where it is unsafe for visitors to travel. The mind is unreal, like a city. It changes overnight. It is peopled by strangers.

Predawn and Ondine awakes, skin slick with the sweat of fever, orgasm, panic. Strasser doesn't know what is wrong. Has her body sensed him in her sleep? Is he a shadow along the wall of a dream, an incubus weight on her chest, Noel Boss patiently smoking in the corner of the room, the rat's-eye cigarette end glowing as he watches her? He tries to hold her, but she fights him off, scratching his neck, pummelling his chest.

"What's wrong?" he asks, but Ondine cannot tell him. She orders him to go, right now, shouting at him when he tries to protest. She barricades herself in the bathroom, and he can hear her breathing heavily and crying great sobs as if she were drowning. There should be something he can do, but it's too fucked up, and maybe it's best just to leave, to leave her alone.

Strasser drives down to the old port and parks near the river. It's almost dawn, but he is too wound up to go back to his apartment. There is a light fog off the water. Soon it will burn off and he will be able to see across. The appointment for Acheson's next interview is in a few hours.

He should back off, stay away from Ondine—he knows that. She is part of the story. She can provide a human angle on the Acheson piece, the struggle he faced, the struggle over the years to find effective treatments. He can use her feelings and observations about the Institute, how the doctors have helped her. But he can't afford to make her more than that.

He'll keep it on-camera—an interview later today or tomorrow—and arrange it for a public place. In an interview Strasser can look at her, listen to the way she talks, try to understand, remain uninvolved. His camera will be a bridge he cannot cross.

The early-morning light is too dark for video; there are only grainy monocolour memories. In Strasser's tape morgue there are videos of Anna, but he doesn't watch them anymore. So much time has passed that he's lost the tracking, images losing focus, oxides realigning. He pursued Anna for three years until finally she agreed to marry. The ceremony was held in a small country church that looked like a Hollywood set. Strasser hired a half-dozen assistants for the day and directed the shoot from the altar. At the wrap party Anna got drunk and caused a scene that didn't make it past the edit. The hour she spent crying in the bathroom was off-camera.

In the pickup interviews the guests said it was a perfect wedding. Even words realign with time, sincere well-wishes now sounding ironic. The marriage lasted a year. Not the first time Strasser has missed the story, misread developments, put the emphasis in the wrong place. He had thought their problems were first-act, but instead it was the end, nothing was scripted past that wedding day. Anna ad-libbed, met someone else, asked for a divorce.

"You'll come back," he predicted.

She did, a year later. It was in December when she called from New York. On the phone she sounded strange, a voice in a dream that calls out so suddenly it wakes you.

"How've you been?" she asked.

"Fine. What time is it?"

"I don't know exactly."

"What's on your mind?"

"I was just wondering," she said, "what's the lethal dose of Valium?"

He flew to New York that morning. It was raining. As the taxi went into midtown, it occurred to Strasser that Anna might not still be alive. He had thought he had heard her cry for help, but she may have only wanted a witness. As the driver complained and the radio phone-in audience bitched about the weather, in the streaming video of the window Strasser saw Anna nude, in a warm bath, a vein exposed like a métro map. Was it the greatest or the least intimacy to find your ex-wife's body?

She was waiting for him in a boutique hotel off Fifth Avenue. "What happened?" he asked.

"I got dumped, that son of a bitch. I was feeling down. Nowhere to go. Everything seemed pointless. I try, but it all fucks up. *I* fuck it up."

"What did you do?"

Anna's voice was like a newspaper report. "I scored some pills. Forty or fifty. Drank some vodka. That was it. It wasn't hard."

She awoke three days later, the sheets clammy with urine. She was thirsty, disoriented. She had a bad headache. She didn't know what to do so she called Strasser.

"I knew you'd be home. You're always home."

"I do go out from time to time."

"Do you?" Anna sounded confused. "I call once and you just happen to be home?"

"I've been out all week. You lucked out."

"Some luck."

She retreated to a corner of the couch, and Strasser got her a glass of water. "Can you tell me what happened?"

"I don't want to talk about it."

She looked puzzled as she sipped the water, as if trying to bring a thought into focus.

"You'll feel better soon. You're just dehydrated."

"You were waiting for me to call." Her voice tried to flirt with him but sounded tired with the effort. "Do you still love me?"

"I don't know," Strasser said. "Sure."

"Will you do me a favour? I need you to hold me. Even if it doesn't mean anything." Her eyes filled with tears. "Even if you don't care."

"All right."

"And turn off the camera."

Strasser goes back to Ondine's apartment and waits outside for an hour, thinking he might see her. He wants to know that she's okay, maybe set up a time to get together later. But when someone finally comes out of the building it is not Ondine but Dr. Kotzwara, looking self-satisfied as he walks briskly to a small Manic GT parked down the street. Strasser follows the doctor as he drives crosstown, then slowly up University Avenue toward the Institute.

TEN

In the underground cave Baum tried to imagine his life in Montreal, but memory was the worst torture. He didn't dare fall asleep or the castration dreams would begin. He experienced delusions. He imagined Dr. Acheson on a Grenfell mission to rescue him. But no one came. Three days passed. Baum may have fainted; he wasn't the hardiest sort, never cut out for the rough-and-tumble. That was why he had gone into medicine. Baum moaned. His ankles were raw with rat bites. There were faces in the dark: Acheson with two men who introduced themselves as Bosch and Schnitzler.

"Stand fast, Herr Baum. We will get you out of this mess."

Baum felt a faint ray of hope. But there was Acheson whispering in his ear like a devil on his shoulder. "Do not trust them," Acheson hissed. "Beware of the mineshaft."

He fainted but was awakened by a sound. Rats? He heard water dripping. He opened his eyes. The old man was pissing on him.

"Where is the bridge?"

Baum didn't understand. London, Brooklyn, Golden Gate? The bridges connecting Montreal to reality? "I haven't seen a bridge—"

The *angakut* began to rave about spirits, wellsprings of the future, the history of a buried people. Baum felt a low rumble rising through his feet and legs as if the bowels of the earth had grown irritable. "The Great Bear," the old man cried, more superstitious bunkum. "The Americans are testing their devices."

Above their heads dirt sifted down and collected in the tunnel. The crossbeam securing Baum's hands cracked like a rifle shot. Baum saw his chance. He slumped forward, working the ropes around the shaman's neck like a garrote. The old man didn't resist. He fell to the floor. Baum scrambled over him, his legs numb and unsteady as he half crawled up the shaft. When he reached the entrance, the light blinded him. He fell to the ground and felt the mine heaving and imploding beneath him. Through the cloud of dust rising he couldn't see if the shaman had escaped. In his panicked flight he never once looked back.

A bush pilot spotted Baum a week later and, alarmed at his condition, flew him to the Mountie detachment in Yellowknife. They shipped him home to Montreal, another southerner gone mad with the view from the top of the world.

At the Institute they never discussed what had happened. Acheson only asked about the notebooks, Baum's record of his experiments. The data must have been satisfactory, for Baum, after a short leave of absence, returned to the Institute with a promotion. He was able to hand over his caseload and concentrate full-time on research. In time he recovered. And yet…

He was uneasy in the dark; he had succubus dreams. In the free-floating time before sleep, Baum would feel images flickering in his preconscious, violent impulses he fought to resist. He immersed himself in work, put in punishing hours, reorganized the lab after a flood that almost shut down the facility. He consulted with governments, published scores of animal studies on rats, always rats. Baum earned the esteem of Acheson, although he privately suspected the general operating director had saddled him with the soubriquet he detested: the Rat Man.

ELEVEN

It was in those start-up years of the Institute, the early fifties. "When did Joseph Stalin die?" Acheson asks. "Was it 1953? I mention it only because it seemed to hold some significance for Dr. Baum."

Strasser stifles a yawn as he adjusts the lighting. "Go on."

"You appear tired, Mr. Strasser. Do you wish to postpone our interview?"

"We only have a couple of more sessions left, Doctor."

"We had just begun a new research program with a chemical that Dr. Baum had isolated from his fieldwork. We were ready to begin limited human experimentation."

Strasser interrupts. "I hoped that today we could talk a little bit about your life outside of medicine. You never married, for instance."

Acheson stares straight ahead, face impassive, impossible for the camera to read. "No." The too-blue eyes stare blankly at the lens like an infinite reflection: no beginning, no end. No questions or answers, only the far-off gaze of television.

"Why not?"

Acheson refocuses, returns to the present. "That is not such an interesting question. It is more curious to know why people do. Do you remember Tolstoy?"

Strasser won't let the doctor distract him. "Have you been in love?"

"I have loved an idea," Acheson says softly, his voice level fibrillating.

"I meant a person, a woman."

"There was a woman."

Strasser sighs. "Do you have any photographs of her?"

Acheson smiles. "You believe that a photograph will tell such a story?"

"A picture is worth—"

"Nothing," Acheson interrupts, voice urgent, almost angry. "Pictures only tell us one type of story. You disagree, yes? You think it is all action! We judge a person by his acts. Is it not so? But you must assess the virtue of a man by his intentions, his dreams. We follow ideas. Obsessions. These, I think, are difficult for one to witness.

"Your camera lies. A man appears in front of you, a very ordinary man. A year later he appears no different. The camera says nothing has changed. But he is not the same person. He has evolved, yes? Perhaps he has regressed. Voices now speak to him. They say terrible things. They say, 'You must kill someone.' They say, 'When the time comes, do not share our secret with anyone.' But the time has not come yet. So the camera is blind. It waits, it says nothing."

"You're talking about killing someone," Strasser says. "The question was: Have you ever been in love?"

"You are quite correct," Acheson says. He pauses for a moment in close-up, his face still. When he finally speaks, Strasser can hear in his voice that something has changed. "It is very curious. I am thinking, Mr. Strasser, that perhaps you would have made an adequate therapist."

They begin again. It was in those start-up years of the Institute, the early fifties. There was a great deal of activity. Dr. Baum was working on isolating an organic compound from a variety of vegetation found only in the Arctic. In this there was nothing unusual. There was interest in all manner of naturally occurring compounds, vegetation, fruit. The scientists at Bayer obtained aspirin from the bark of a willow tree.

"You may ask why a tree would produce something to cure headaches," Acheson asks. "We do not know. Perhaps there was a reason once, but we have forgotten it. Or we are meant to be curious, like the cat. Perhaps there is no reason. It is God's little joke."

"Who was the woman?"

Acheson starts slowly, describing himself at an age when affairs, infatuations, were more than mere memories, things of the past. There were brief interludes, to be sure, but largely he was spared the *Sturm und Drang* of love. He did not remember the details that enable love to take root, the faces of the beloved long since crowded out by the many patients he had seen. In this there was no tragedy. A life is not a continuous road; it suffers detours, strays over unmapped terrain. We wish it to pass from A to B, but that is vanity, the analysis retrospective. We stop for gas and speak to a woman. Will we recall her face a hundred miles hence? To what end, what purpose? After the dislocations of two wars, after fleeing Germany and Switzerland, what photographs could memory bring ashore?

Mary P. was young when he first encountered her, only twenty-three, and the differences in their ages struck him as absurd. She was a handsome woman in a delicate way, and he admired the way she tried to master her agitation as she sat across from him. During that first interview, she betrayed certain mannerisms—a nervous tic that afflicted her left eye, an alarm reaction if a voice were raised—that indicated her home life was not a peaceful one; it was, in fact, a battleground.

The interview with her husband confirmed Acheson's suspicions. Mr. P. was a belligerent, ill-natured man with thick, hirsute hands. His brow suggested low intelligence and a violent tendency. It was inconceivable that Mary would feel attraction for such a man and, indeed, she showed no warmth when she spoke of him. There were no signs of abuse, although there was a bruise on her inner thigh and slight vaginal tearing suggestive of a rather powerful coupling. Mary did not complain of these injuries; indeed, after much hesitation, she reported that relations with her husband were vigorous, but did not appear dissatisfied. This suggested denial and an unhealthy dependence on her husband's brand of physical love. It was imperative for her own safety that Mary be removed from his influence at the earliest possible moment.

"I'm afraid your condition will only worsen if your present situation does not change," Acheson told her. "You are tired, under considerable stress. I have arranged for a bed in the hospital for you. It should only be for a short time."

She seemed to greet the news with relief. She thanked him for his attentions, returned his smile before slipping out of the office.

TWELVE

Ondine awakens at noon in a benzo haze, groggy, can't clear her head in the hypnopomp. Through the glare of a headache she sees herself on location in Newfoundland, sundown slanting off the water giving a flat perspective, Technicolor red, vermilion or demillean, colours seen only in movies. There is something going on just out of the frame. She turns, pans right. Strasser is the camera-man inside her head.

Zoom in on a campfire in a small copse where some kind of ritual dance is being performed. Shawnadithit is there, her body painted red. She holds for a close-up: *"Delood. Ejew theehone."*

She lies down by the fire in a shallow trench. A strange bearded man steps into the firelight and seats himself behind her head. He stares into the fire. "Tell me, what is it that you dream?"

"I am a flame rising up into the night sky."

"Flying, yes? *Gen italien?* To Italy?"

Shawnadithit becomes angry. She does not understand this interpretation. What is Italy? Is it a place?

No, it is the *genitalien* dream of Eros. Sigmund smiles, although his well-admired humour is lost on this girl.

She shakes her head vigorously. Not Eros, but the Other. She rises. She wants this to end. But Sigmund will not allow her to leave, insists she return the next night, the night after that. He will measure out her life in fifty-minute spans. He is shaman. She is bound to him. He takes a stick from the fire and draws a symbol in the dirt: it is infinity. It is twin shackles. It is a chemical formula of a drug he has prepared. It is *Dagaz*, the rune of transformation.

In September 1828 it was decided that the redskin woman Shawnadithit, being one of the last of a tribe extirpated, should be returned to St. John's for her safety and education. Upon her arrival she was installed in the home of William Cormack, who had lately crossed the interior in search of her people. He was a gentle, caring man, and Shawnadithit kept house for the kindly bachelor as if she were his woman, preparing his meals as he sat near the fire patiently teaching her English.

All that season as autumn lengthened and chill winds gathered over the Atlantic she passed the hours with Cormack. She drew pictures to explain the story of her people: how they lived and hunted, the weapons they used, the places they lived. She spoke of man and woman. She told of the Beothuk deities and the mad missionaries who had tried to uproot them. Cormack kept records, detailed notes. He questioned Shawnadithit about the sun god Kuis, the burial rites of the Beothuks, the painting of the dead with red ochre, beliefs and customs he knew from his travels to have originated in ancient Egypt. Other customs of her people were similar to those seen in Pacific tribes along the British Columbia coast and across to Siberia. "I have discovered," Cormack wrote in a letter discovered among his effects, "an ancient truth that has been forgotten by our people but which has been known and preserved for centuries by the Beothuk."

At Christmastime he bought her small gifts delicately wrapped: bright cloth to make clothes, sewing needles, spun candy, a pendant once worn by his mother. "For many years it has been in our family," he told her. "It is only right and just that you should wear it."

Shawnadithit did not understand. What was the meaning of his words? Cormack said no more. Instead he withdrew most anxiously from her view and retired to his room. He did not ask her to lay a fire there but bolted his door. When Shawnadithit retired later that night, she heard Cormack at his writing desk, the coarse scratch of a pen. The light under his door burned like fever.

III

The shifting of memory patterns is basic to psychotherapy.
——Dr. Helen Noel

...the psychic life in some mental diseases...is constricted
to a very small circle of thoughts, which master all others,
recurring again and again in the sick brain...
——Dr. Egaz Moniz

ONE

As Mary P. took her nightly pill, she felt a heat, an oceanic surge, as if all of her desires were issuing from her body and warming the room, melting the walls of resistance and reserve, thawing the chilled heart.

Then the doctor would arrive. He would come to her bedside and inquire about her health, her mood, touch her forehead, feel her pulse. "Have you taken your medication this evening, Mary?"

Mary P. would nod. "Yes."

Perhaps there would be a gift, a piece of fruit, a gramophone on which he would play sad recordings, mostly operas, usually in German. Then he would perch on the edge of her bed and take her hand and together they would listen to the music. Mary was alone for much of the day, and she began to look forward to these nightly visits. On a few occasions Dr. Acheson would try to explain the opera's story, but she scarcely listened. Even if she did not understand the words, she heard the voices crying, she knew the passion in their hearts.

In the hours they spent together it was perhaps unusual for the doctor to hold her hand, but Mary felt little urge to resist. In the papery dryness of his touch there was something written that she understood. Her sense of empathy was acute; the medication he administered helped her with that.

He questioned her about the drug he had prescribed, if it eased her fatigue, helped her feel less anxious? Yes, and more. She explained the warmth, how even in the faces of strangers she saw nothing to fear. She sensed great strength. She had no appetite. She felt as if she were in love. She wanted to hold the body of the world and press it to her breast. "It's absurd, I know," she said. "But don't say anything, Doctor. Don't spoil it."

He kissed her hand then; she felt the light stubble of his lip. "What do you desire? If there's anything..."

"Home. I want to be with my husband."

There can be no edifice on a foundation of sand, nothing trusted to the rotten ghosts of memory, the shift of desire. Dr. Acheson was forced to admit that his little experiment was a failure. The environment he created for Mary P. was not enough; it was a vacation spot, a honeymoon. Acheson lifted the needle and slipped the 78 of Wagner into the sleeve. "Just a little while longer, Mary," he said, "but first you will need rest."

In his flight from Germany the bar girl Lola-Lola aka Werther Acheson was rumoured to have been accompanied by Adam aka X.

"Was Ondine ever given this drug?" Strasser asks.

"I wish I could tell you," Kotzwara says, some equivocation there. "But it was just a starting point. There are other compounds, much more powerful." He shrugs. "You hear so many things. Come, walk with me. I only have a few minutes. We're about to run an experiment with one of our test subjects."

"Mind if I watch?"

"Bring your friend," Kotzwara says, nodding to the camera, "but I don't know if there's anything you can use."

Strasser tracks along the corridor as Kotzwara gives the skinny on Adam, cousin of more famous amphetamines, a poor relation that lacked the kick of crank. At the Darmstadt lab the Merck *menschen* made a halfhearted attempt to market Adam as an appetite suppressant, but dieting wasn't a popular fad. Even Dietrich herself was full-figured in her *Blaue Engel* Apotheke days.

"It was a drug, you see, that didn't seem to have any useful effect," Kotzwara says.

"How can you make money from a medicine that doesn't do anything?" Strasser asks.

"Patent medicines, homeopathy, vitamins. Better stick to media punditry, Mr. Strasser. But I concede that most people wouldn't have bothered with it. Isn't that the nature of genius—understanding the significance of something before it can be perceived? Dr. Acheson always had a grasp of the bigger picture. He understood that once an idea has formed it can never die, only get transformed. That's our curse—genocide, Total War, the Bomb, ideas that come to us like nightmares we can't forget. They'll be with us forever." One of the principles of psychodynamics, the conservation of paranoia.

"There's another side to it," Strasser points out.

"There always is," Kotzwara concedes. He knows that paranoia's just the B-side of the search for knowledge. "Universal peace, love and understanding. We can dream up utopias. But even if we get there, will it be worth the unhappiness it has already caused?"

Adam dropped out of favour during the war until the 1950s when, like Frank Sinatra, he staged a comeback. Few saw his true potential. He was sold as a lowly cough suppressant in 1958 under a U.S. patent, as a tranquillizer in England, then stateside again as a diet pill. All the while Acheson was conducting his own experiments along radically different lines.

"Ondine said that Adam can stimulate emotions," Strasser says.

"Stimulate or simulate. Who knows? I've heard rumours that

Dr. Acheson played the orgone circuit in his younger days. Back in the sixties he even dragged Dr. Baum into it. Frankly the two of them should have given it a rest. But Acheson wouldn't drop the idea. He was lonely, poor man. It clouds judgement. Of course, it was mad to meddle in this whole business, but there you have it. He didn't see it that way. I attended a lecture of his once, quite remarkable. Something to do with the chemical libido, Jung's energy of life."

There was Adam, ghost of desire, circling the globe like an unclaimed package that Acheson wanted to bring to earth. "Of course, Adam wasn't perfect, original sin and all that," Kotzwara says. "Had a bit of a nasty side-effect profile. Not surprisingly, it makes the blood boil—clotting irregularities, kidney problems. Not too bad if you pop the subject into a deep freeze—chill-out rooms I believe they call them now—but it's not an ideal arrangement. We're always looking for new compounds. Which is why Dr. Acheson packed one of the lads—Baum, do you know him?—off to the Territories as far back as the fifties. The man was always looking ahead."

"Why the Territories?"

"Ultima Thule, if you believe the stories. That's where you'll find the Other. Think of all the opiates—heroin and the like—clicking into receptors in the brain. You might ask yourself why? Why do our brains have opiate receptors? Why should our brains respond to a chemical that's fairly uncommon in our environment, doesn't do a damned bit of good for our survival instinct. The simple answer: the lock opens because we must already have the key. What is that key? It's a shadow. But it led to the hypothesis that if our brains have opiate receptors, we must manufacture our own opiates. Which is how they discovered endorphins. At the time it was a rather radical notion, that somewhere out there in the laboratory of the world were the keys to unlock the mind."

For Baum it must have seemed more of a mad quest. Under the cranial sky the flare of the aurora borealis must have looked like an electromagnetic manifestation of unrequited love, the ionosphere sparking with failed romances, unvoiced thoughts, the lonely staccato of Morse code chattering across the barren lands. How was he to know there was no love here only failure, the acid taste of humiliation.

"You make it sound as if emotions are just something you cook up in chemistry class," Strasser objects.

"Neurochemistry," Kotzwara says. "Did you think it was more than that?"

Two

S trasser lugs his gear to an observation room adjoining the para-philia lab while Kotzwara settles in to read the zero-wave EEG tracings as if they were tea leaves.

"I wanted to ask you about Ondine," Strasser says. "I saw you coming out of her place."

An intercom interrupts. "We're ready, Doctor."

"I'm needed in the lab," Kotzwara says. "You can set up in there. Try to be unobtrusive."

Strasser shoulders the camera and follows the doctor into the lab. In the centre of the room is a man in his mid-twenties: track pants, training shoes, chest bare, one nipple pierced. "I'll need a waiver," Strasser says.

"If you see a waver, don't wave back," Kotzwara jokes before turning to the young man. "We're going to tape this session, Terry."

Terry is unconcerned, nods briefly as he slips his pants down to his ankles and wrestles with a lab assistant for a tub of electrolyte gel.

"This is Justine," Kotzwara says. "Justine, please try to control your subject."

Justine seems on the brink of losing her professional cool, this tech day job just a way to pay her way through night training in Shepardian fornicotherapy. "The subject isn't cooperating." She straightens up, tucks away the peek of a black brassiere strap, man-handles Terry onto a tilt table, and fixes the restraints. Then she applies a series of electrodes to Terry's exposed penis, now slick with gel and ready to assume grotesque proportions.

"Get ready," Kotzwara warns Strasser. "We're about to initiate the vertical-restraint apparatus."

"I don't know if I can use this."

"As I said…"

"What's the point of this experiment?"

"Frame it head-and-shoulders," Kotzwara orders. "I'll explain it as we go along."

Strasser watches as Justine lowers a rubber halter and positions it around Terry's neck, tightening it as the subject squirms and shifts on the table.

Kotzwara smiles. "Today in the noose…"

Strasser turns the camera off. "You aren't," he asks, confused, "planning to strangle him, are you?"

"That's it precisely."

"I don't understand."

"'I have been half in love with easeful Death,'" Kotzwara quotes. "A little Keats to set the mood." He pauses, eyes studying Strasser through a bifocal plane. "You mustn't be so anxious, Mr. Strasser. You're looking a little pale. Perhaps you'd like to take something?"

"I'm fine, Doctor," Strasser says, ducking back behind the camera. "Rolling."

Kotzwara starts talking in a fusty BBC style he's acquired from nights listening to the World Service sparking off the ionosphere. "The purpose of the experiment is to re-create the environment of the paraphiliac, one of our many research interests at the Institute. The current study is examining the phenomenon of sexual strangulation—that is, strangulation to achieve or intensify the sexual experience. You may recall certain rumours about a pop star down in Australia? I should emphasize, mind you, that this behaviour isn't new. There are many examples throughout history, dating back at least as far as the Reverend Manacle…"

Cut away to the Reverend Manacle, who first recorded the phenomenon while tending to his flock in prison. One of his tasks in ministering to the fallen was to serve as witness at executions, a duty he could only bear by assuming a certain clinical mien and the pose of close observation. As the prisoners dangled at the end of the rope, their hands shackled with eponymous restraints, Manacle dryly recorded what had been apparent to many of the spectators of the gentler sex: the men would inevitably display a certain tumescence.

It was an observation that obsessed him, consumed his pitiable sleep and brought unwelcome warmth to his marital bed, cold now these many years. The reverend, it was said, while still a man if not in the spring of youth then in its early autumn, had endured an uncharitable impotence that had persisted like a plague. In that time he had seen his home life decline and converse with his wife, once so gentle and sweet, suffer an unmistakable tartness. "My gentle husband, and soft," she would say to him. Or amid the passion of argument: "You unhorsed stallion, you soft-finned cod, you knackless knacker." And so on.

And yet the reverend's desires, it may be said, were not absent, only mightily bound. In his journal Manacle confessed he imagined a woman of low repute—a slattern, barmaid, slut—who would break his unmanly bonds, unchain his unspeakable desire.

After an especially unquiet row, the reverend resolved to perform an experiment, one that required securing the services of a prostitute. The reverend's wrists were bound and the woman attached a cord to his neck. Veins bulging, face red and apoplectic, Manacle struggled and gasped for breath. Mistress of the Night! Mercy!

It is unclear if the reverend would have continued this game until death. No matter. For behold: the long-dormant penis arose like a Leviathan from the depths, whereupon the good reverend fucked the young maid *ex animalis* until her lips turned blue.

"We have reports of the same sorts of things among North and South American Native tribes, ancient Greeks," Kotzwara says, still in BBC mode. "The Mayans reserved a special place in paradise watched over by Ixtab, goddess of the hanged." The doctor turns on the EEG; at zero the ink marks like scratches across a naked back. With the signal established, a baseline brain-wave pattern begins to form like ghost writing. But there is no response, the reading on Terry's penile graph as unimpressive as, well, a penis.

Then Justine hits a button and the rubber halter slowly lifts Terry out of his chair. The penile graph stirs as Terry starts to grimace. "Oh, my God. Oh, my God, Doc…"

"Terry's a disinhib—too many nights falling asleep in front of the TV," Kotzwara says. "The mind's receptive during sleep and the signals get in, burn out parts of the brain."

"Still," Strasser says, noting Terry is now well-hung and hanging, "doesn't that hurt him?"

"Does that sound to you like a man in pain?"

Through the lens Terry is starting to fly, now about six inches off the chair with a full erection.

"Even so," Strasser says.

"I assure you we do take the precaution of measuring the pressure inside the halter. Just in case."

"Oh, yeah, that's so good, that feels so good, Doc…"

"In case of what?"

"Mishaps have been known to occur." Like the Reverend Manacle himself during a rather self-indulgent session, *les petits morts* only mild temblors before the Big One. "Pressure on the carotid sinus can stimulate the vagus nerve. The heart slows down and the patient dies of sudden death."

"Kind of rough."

"That's how they like it," Kotzwara says. "The learning curve in this sort of enterprise is much like a precipice, as you can imagine. So much ritual involved with these paraphiliacs, they don't always want to share the knowledge with the uninitiated. We're only scientists. They're the true devotees."

Some false modesty here; Kotzwara's been known to attach a nipple clamp or two on his weekly sojourns to the leather bars trolling for subjects. He finds more than enough volunteers, the psych lab setup offering a turn at the electroshock apparatus, which Kotzwara has had adapted for use on penises and nipples. Most recently he's been known to haunt the Très Cuir bar off St-Denis with a couple of the boys from the Institute: Collins the manqué; Eigenvalue the Max Factor fetishist.

Collins: "I'm in a long dark tunnel, damp walls, light at the end of. There's a sewer rat. I get anxious. I see he has an enormous penis."

Kotzwara: "Interesting. Are you sure it's a penis? It's not an umbrella?"

Collins: "I'm the one with the umbrella. But it won't open."

Kotzwara: "Very interesting."

A little tedious really, these long evenings of shoptalk, but the docs only travel in packs now, always a little paranoid about what's going on out there in the real world.

"Justine," Kotzwara says, "we're picking up some interference in one of the leads. See what you can do."

"Right," Justine replies, and hits the panic switch. The rubber halter eases off, lowering Terry back onto the table, a hydraulic sigh that may be from Terry or the machine.

"A fascinating *unterwelt*," Kotzwara comments. "Step into that world and it's sometimes hard to know what's going on." He pauses, waits for Strasser to shut down the camera, audio, too. This is, of course, strictly background...

Cut to Kotzwara at a joint on the Main watching a Mademoiselle Maplune, a somewhat witchy *belle dame sans merci* and bit-part actress on a television courtroom drama. Told Kotzwara she'd get off at three or promised she would, invited the doctor to her fourth-floor walkup with an offer of a good time, Kotzwara naturally curious about the paraphiliac pleasures of barbed-wire brassieres. "With bracelets too and fragrant zone"—more Keatsian kitsch. Not so fragrant as it turned out, but the barbed wire and bracelets were real enough. Kotzwara stripped down to his very attractive leather thong and was effectively immobilized when out of the next room came Terry, intent on relieving him of his cash and credit cards.

"I am a doctor, young man," Kotzwara said, trying to keep voice and member equally impressive as he eyed Terry's gun. "Dr. Kotzwara. I must caution you that you're ruining the therapeutic alliance."

Terry told him to stow it. He wasn't about to listen—as he said in what would become a famous phrase—to any Kotzwaran kaka. He brandished the pistol—my God, is that a Luger! how delicious—gesturing at the portion of Kotzwara's belly that overflowed his thong.

Kotzwara was renowned for keeping his cool with a gun to his head. He had employed one once himself—a rather pretty 9 mm semiautomatic—while treating a woman with such powerful unconscious guilt that she resisted every attempt at therapy. The patient's masochistic neuroses—what Freud would have called her "need for punishment"—made her relish her own unwellness. Something had to be done but quick. Kotzwara drew his piece. The results were not entirely unrewarding. The woman claimed she was cured and was never seen again. And for a brief time Kotzwara enjoyed a small fame around the Institute—"When I hear neurosis, I pull out my gun"—although he was dissuaded by Dr. Baum from repeating the experiment.

Such clinical curios would cut no slack with Terry; Kotzwara could see that. "Are you planning," the doctor asked, his voice only breaking slightly, "to kill me?"

"It ain't half of what your kind deserves."

Kotzwara saw an opening and seized it. "Tell me, what do I deserve?"

Such chutzpah took Terry by surprise; for a second he felt his imagination under challenge. What to do, what to do? "I oughta," he struggled for a moment, "I oughta strap a cage of live rats to your ass and let them dig their way out."

"Gross," Maplune said. By this time she was chafing to go home, relax, maybe slip into something even less comfortable. Terry was tripping into some stuff here that she didn't want to know about. "M'moune," she prickled, "get the money and let's get the fuck out of here."

But Terry wouldn't be silenced. "Would you like that, Doctorman? You want a live rat up your ass?"

"Funny you should say that," Kotzwara said.

THREE

Ondine pauses at the door of an antique shop on Notre-Dame. "They really aren't antiques, Ondine," Bill Mannekin protests. "They're scarcely collectibles. Junk, really."

Ondine ignores him and disappears into the store. Mannekin sighs. If he hadn't blown that restaurant gig, he wouldn't be schlepping all over town, following in the wake of Ondine's mad pursuit of...what?

He enters the store, careful not to touch anything. Old objects were writ large with a spectral signature, the graffito of the dispossessed. The city was lousy with memory. But kitsch interfered with the true vibrations, the rare artifacts that glowed with a spectral aura. The location signal of the past was becoming overwhelmed: souvenir ashtrays, record stands, aluminum picnic coolers, the mass clutter that is the mass unconscious, cycling and recycling, never dying.

He doesn't know what Ondine is searching for, but he's sure they won't find it here. The junk shops and jumble sales are cirrus, false vapour trails. There is no immanence, though Ondine wants to believe there is. He knows she will find nothing of value, nothing that can conjure any details of Shawnadithit's life. Women vanish from history like lost love: telephone number delisted, name changed to a married alias. Impossible to locate other than through gossip, rumour, improbable speculation.

Ondine wants trees, a restful place, but she won't go up to the park on the mountain. They go to a smaller spot in the west end and find a quiet copse of pines. Ondine closes her eyes and tries to feel them in the shift of air: Shawnadithit's mother and sister, their dead voices whispering in the boughs. It is a scene that Mannekin once described to her.

After Shawna's final move to St. John's, perhaps the voices were louder, more persuasive. William Cormack didn't hear them. He was deaf to the world of the spirit, blind to the way she looked at him. As they sat over her drawings, she would touch his arm, but he would retreat into himself, taking refuge in some lonely, quiet place where she couldn't accompany him. He asked about her nightly trips to the woods, and she brought him there, into the bower where she would speak to her family and breathe their sense of peace.

It was near Christmas, with the snow as deep as the day her father had died, that Shawnadithit felt him step in close behind her, circling her waist with his arms. But he slipped away before she could turn and trudged back across the field alone.

"What did she feel, Bill?" Ondine asks, but Mannekin can't say. He has sensed her *sentiment d'incomplétude*, has tried to fill it. He told her the story of the spirit-speak—the late-night visitations, communicating with the dead—because it felt right. It was what she wanted to hear. It was a ready-made, something invented on the spur of the moment, but she has never forgotten it. On numerous occasions she has asked him to repeat it. Like a child, she protests if the details ever change. The story seems to calm her.

"Did they talk to her about what it was going to be like? Death, I mean."

"When we try to imagine our own death, we always survive as a spectator. I think Freud told me that once."

"Do you believe it?"

"I believe that when Shawna visited the woods at night she saw the Shadow," Mannekin intones, "the history of the Unconscious."

"But they told her? About death?"

"I think so, yes. I like to think she heard the future whispering to her. It is possible. Curved space, the past is the future."

"Don't," Ondine protests. "You make it sound like a *Star Trek* episode."

"That only proves my point. They stopped broadcasting that show back in '69. Except the signal leaked into space, circled the universe, and came back to Earth. Now it's showing up everywhere. I keep picking up that 'Dagger of the Mind' episode on my crystal ball."

Ondine has to laugh, something she hasn't done in a long time.

"The future's like a giant TV screen," Mannekin continues. "Some great historical epic, a cast of thousands, a little cramped but digitally remastered for our viewing pleasure."

"Is that your vision?" Ondine teases. "You think history's a Cecil B. DeMille film fest?"

"Something like that. Mannekin enjoys seeing her smile and decides not to tell her what else he sees, the narration track on the videodisc. One surgical strike, a thermonuclear cathartic, could erase everything, obliterating the memory of the universe. It is in position; he can feel its laser tip even now ready to descend…

Ondine lies back on the grass, blinded, staring up at the sky. "Sometimes, Bill, I think I can really understand what happened." She sits up abruptly. "I mean what *really* happened."

He doesn't ask her to explain. Over the past few weeks it has become clear to Mannekin that the image she is searching for—free-floating just out of reach like a postcard under a crystal ball—is from Ondine's past, not Shawnadithit's. He watches her lie back, shielding her eyes from the sun. Mannekin is no therapist. It's not his job to exorcise demons.

Ondine doesn't speak for a long time. "Bill," she asks at last, "do you think people in the future are trying to communicate with us?"

"Yes."

"Why?"

"So we'll change."

"Why would they want that?" Ondine asks. "If we change, we'll alter the future. Why would people in the future want to change the way things turned out?"

"Maybe they didn't turn out," Mannekin says. At moments like these he can feel that burden of history bearing down on him, the truth and lies indistinguishable, the lives as manufactured and banal as kewpie dolls. "Maybe we don't survive."

FOUR

So Kotzwara was doing the Scheherazade routine, trussed like Tom Turkey and talking a blue streak. "I think, Terry, that it would be helpful if you shared your fantasies with us."

"Shut the fuck up," la belle Maplune said. "Don't let him start messing with your head."

"This fantasy of the rat," Kotzwara continued, "is this something you saw in a dream or is it an event from your experience?"

The question made Terry hesitate. "I don't know," he said, lowering himself onto a chair. "A dream, I guess."

"You needn't feel ashamed," Kotzwara reassured him. "There's a rather famous story of someone who was bothered by the same image."

Seems that once there was this troubled chap who went to see Professor Freud in October 1907. Freud dubbed him *die Rattenmann*, although his real name was Ernst Lanzer.

As a young boy, Lanzer had been obsessed with seeing women naked. The "little voluptuary," as Freud called him, distinctly remembered feeling pleasure as he watched his pretty governess at night squeezing out the quite sizable boils on her buttocks. It was, Kotzwara noted, the only recorded case of abscessional neurosis.

The sessions with Freud lasted eleven months. Lanzer revealed a wealth of repressed material. The complexity of the case left Freud feeling overwhelmed. He didn't think he would ever be able to explain the case fully. His colleague Jung agreed. In a letter to Sandor Ferenczi, he wrote: "Dear S.: Freud's case of the Rat Man is very hard to understand. I will soon have to read it for the third time. Am I especially stupid?"

The sessions ended, but Lanzer remained disturbed throughout adolescence. He masturbated frequently, in the afterglow feeling an intense, inexplicable aggression. He wished his father were dead. In time he became engaged, but this deviation into normalcy proved only to be the calm before the storm. During the engagement, his fiancée was called away to attend her sick grandmother. Lanzer became enraged. He thought: "I should like to go and kill that old woman for robbing me of my love." Then he heard a second voice: "Kill *yourself* as a punishment for these savage and murderous passions!"

Who said that? Was that his dick speaking? As punishment, he spent the rest of the night beating it. Then the inevitable period of contrition. When his fiancée returned, he tried to seduce her. At the peak of their foreplay she cried out, "*O! Der Dicke!*" meaning "the fat boy." Lanzer was horrified; he withdrew and was unable to continue. He resolved in his obsessive way to lose weight at once. He began taking diet pills, amphetamines, that he had stolen from the local hospital.

Was Lanzer obese, or did he suffer from a body-dysmorphic delusion? Hard to say. There may have been a misunderstanding. Seems that in recent months Lanzer's fiancée had been spending an undue amount of time with her cousin from England, one Richard Andere. The other Dick.

Lanzer was wracked, if you will, with jealousy. The inevitable crisis came to a head during a holiday. Lanzer and his fiancée argued violently. He could stand no more. In despair Lanzer turned and ran away from her along a mountain path. He arrived breathless at the summit, amphetamine blood booming in his head. As he stared out at the ocean, he was seized by a sudden impulse to throw himself over the precipice like a lemming.

Lanzer survived, the engagement was broken off. The young man's symptoms appeared to go into remission until the age of twenty-six when he finally lost his virginity. He would later tell Dr. Acheson that he remembered lying in the postcoital quiet smoking a cigarette and thinking, "This is glorious! One might murder one's father for this!"

Back online at the Institute and Terry is sweating bullets trying to ejaculate, but it's no good. Justine watches like a schoolmarm, horned-rim glasses teetering on the tip of her nose. It's another variable Kotzwara has factored in. Seems the horny librarian shtick is on Terry's fantasy top ten. Justine smiles pure vamp; she's enjoying the subject's distress. She struts across the frame and takes up a position behind Terry's right ear. "You're pathetic," she murmurs dominatrix-style, "hanging there just *dying* to fuck me up the ass, you miserable piece of shit." Which is just enough for Terry to reach superthreshold.

"Justine," Kotzwara shouts irritably, "lay off the verbal stimuli."

"I was just—"

"All right, all right," he says with fatigue as he shuts down the apparatus. "Just record everything you said to the subject. And I want a full report from Terry on his recalled reactions."

"More variables?" Strasser asks.

"The world is ill," Kotzwara says, "and I get the job of recording it."

"Ditto."

"This particular analysis is going to be a bitch. Eigenvalue's going to have my head. We've got submission content, anal eroticism, sodomy. Language is just too goddamned messy. It's going to take months to sort this shit out."

Strasser turns off the camera. "Don't say 'shit.' It gets me hot."

Kotzwara manages a laugh. "Add coprophilia to the list of variables. You may as well put in aggression while you're at it."

"I don't understand."

"Something we've picked up from our previous series," Kotzwara says, folding up the EEG trace like an accordion. "Sex and aggression appear to be paired responses. Look at Lanzer, hot under the collar and wanting to kill himself or murder his father. What's the connection between sex and death?" Kotzwara shrugs—another question for another day. "It's not just us. We've even noticed the phenomenon in our experiments with rats."

"Rats?" Terry says, one leg dangling freeze-frame in his track pants. "I'll go again, Doc, if you tell me about the rats…"

The story of the rats, as it turned out, may just have saved Kotzwara's thonged ass. As Terry and Maplune settled in, Kotzwara told them the circumstances of Lanzer's relapse after he was sent back to the front. The day had been punctuated by explosions all along the line. One shell had collapsed the tunnel, trapping Lanzer in a mountain of shit. It had taken the other men an hour to dig him out. When they found him, Lanzer was lodged in a large cooking pot. As the men pried him out, the captain—always something of a raconteur—mused about a form of punishment used in the Orient. A man was tied up, a pot was filled with rats and turned upside down on his ass. The rats would bore their way into his anus, following the tunnel up into the light.

Strasser recalls something Dr. Acheson told him during one of his interviews: *Lanzer particularly enjoyed scenes with rats in them, in the tenements, in the sin holes and streets.* He mentions it to Kotzwara. "Were the rats symbolic?"

"Why not?" Kotzwara says amiably. "The rat as mother, father, alien influence invading the home. Dirt, evil, contagion. Did the rats represent himself—'In the bloated rat he sees a likeness'? The bloated Mr. Lanzer would have known his Goethe. Rats as shit, rats as money—Freud's personal favourite, going on and on about the *Spielratte*, Lanzer's father being something of a gambler. Then there's 'hanging a rat,' the rat as penis."

"Which is it?"

"Any of them, or none." Kotzwara smiles apologetically, on a bit of a jag. "Sometimes a rat is just a rat."

FIVE

R ats in the alley, rats in the bower, rats on shore from a sinking ship. To dream of a rat is to be deceived, to dream of plague means your lover will create misery.

On the water she sees a boat cleaving the waves, hull hissing like ancient celluloid. Something borrowed from Murnau, Lang, Pabst, a film image as jittery as she is. Ondine feels anxiety closing in, her thoughts ratcheting in black and white toward that same inevitable conclusion. She closes her eyes, cut to black, but even here there is a title card: *"And when he had crossed the bridge, the phantoms came to meet him…"* In the dark, waiting for her at the gate is Max Schreck, the Nosferatu come to bleed her.

◈

"I saw you this morning coming out of Ondine's apartment," Strasser tells Kotzwara. "I wanted to ask—"

"You were there?"

"Did she mention?"

"We talked about a lot of things. She was quite upset, nocturnal panic attack." Kotzwara looks out the window to the mountain slope, away from Strasser, the office set dressed in Tex-Mex decor, Western saddle, serape, stirrups. "Are you involved with her?"

"Is she capable?"

"Are you? Or is this just part of the story you're putting together?"

"Last night was different."

"Always the same difference."

"There's something about her I don't understand."

Kotzwara smiles. "Inevitably."

"What set her off?" Strasser asks. "Was it something I said? What started this thing?"

"There are many different triggers."

"She said she was at school when she had the first attack."

"*Had* the attack? Is that what she said?"

Mary P. developed resistance to therapy, asked the nurse to remove the gramophone, was silent and withdrawn when Acheson visited her at night. The doctor no longer tried to touch her—that was progress. She wanted to shut out his voice when he spoke to her about her husband. He wasn't openly critical, clever bastard. He insinuated. He offered asides: perhaps Mr. P. wasn't the best husband, perhaps he was prone to violence and would hurt her one day. Acheson analyzed their exchanges, what her husband had said to her, even the soft words spoken in private. He seemed to be competing on some field of honour, and everything she had told him in their sessions, every word, was ammunition.

She fought him. She resisted. She talked often about having children, but Acheson heard only her inner voice crying for rebirth.

She asked that he allow Mr. P. to visit, pleaded, demanded. He confined her to her room. She barred the door with a chair, refusing him entry even when she heard him weeping. She had had enough. She wanted to go back into the world. Acheson expressed sympathy but told her it was quite impossible. An early release, he cautioned, might produce relapse; he prescribed rest.

The following morning Mary began her REST, regressive electroshock therapy, three Page-Russell treatments a day. After the first series, she experienced severe muscle spasms and couldn't move from her bed for three days. When she recovered, a second series was begun. A muscle relaxant was prescribed to prevent any further physical injury. To her regimen Acheson added microdoses of a novel psychotomimetic compound Baum had isolated in Yellowknife. It had slight hallucinogenic properties, yes, but it was a useful agent to free the mind of its preconceptions, biases, shackles of personality. The future otherwise so fated, limited by the brain itself, its small capacity to dream.

"We are making significant progress," Acheson informed Mr. P. "I am greatly encouraged."

But progress wasn't as rapid as Acheson had hoped; he needed to do more. He needed to enter the depths of her thoughts and lead her back. He needed to isolate her from other influences—radio, TV, conversation, external stimuli. So at night Mary was required to wear a football helmet, which confined her head and allowed her to hear tapes Acheson had made from their sessions together.

"You understand that you are not well."

"Are not well."

"It is very important for your therapy that you believe this. You want to get well, don't you? You want to leave this place?"

"Yes."

"This is for your own good. You know that everyone in the hospital cares about you. The nurses care about you. I care about you."

The tape hisses like an ocean tide receding. *"I care about you."*

"No, you don't—"

"Listen: I care about you. Repeat."

"You care about me."

"I want you to be happy."

"You care about me and want me to be happy."

"Repeat."

"You care about me and want me to be happy."

"Good." The tape was edited and replayed a thousand times a day like an SOS from outer space.

"You care about me and want me to be happy."

"You care about me and want me to be happy."

"You care about me and want me to be happy."

Mary became withdrawn, uncommunicative. She had difficulty sleeping. She complained of being depressed. She couldn't concentrate, the taped voices playing continuously now so she couldn't collect her thoughts. She became confused, didn't know if it was day or night, was uncertain where she was. It always went like that: time, place, personality. That was how things are lost. That is how the mind recedes.

"Is it time for lunch or dinner?"

She was uncertain.

"Where are you?"

She didn't know.

"Who are you?"

"I want to go home."

It was necessary to increase the number of taped repetitions to five thousand a day. Mary wasn't permitted to remove the helmet. The tape played while she ate, slept, took the air in the gardens behind the Institute. The flowers reminded her of beds of roses, peonies, mums—"I remember that Mr. P. always loved…"

She clung to the past, to Mr. P. So more medication was prescribed, more Page-Russells. The staff commented on Acheson's persistence. Another doctor would have given up—diagnosis refractory—and moved on. But Acheson was a patient man. It took time to change a person, to discard the chrysalis of personality. He knew patients could show a surprising tenacity in clinging to their beliefs about themselves.

"You understand that I care about you."

"You care."

"I love you."

"Yes."

"Repeat."

She listened to the tape ten thousand times a day. Buffeted by wave upon wave, words repeated endlessly so that they meant nothing, she no longer recognized the voice as her own: it was wind, interference, static.

"Do you understand the process?" Acheson asks Strasser. "We are at war, each against the other. We must find a mate, yes? So our minds are constructed to seek novelty, someone different from ourselves. But that very differentness causes us anxiety. Opposites attract, but we may not find happiness if we cannot shed that strangeness. The marriage project is to join with the other, to become a common identity. There is no 'you' or 'me,' only 'us.' We are only happy when we surrender our identity. Otherwise there is disharmony, friction."

"But her identify was erased," Strasser says. "There was nothing there."

"As we are in the beginning, in every birth and rebirth." Acheson remembers even now how smooth her brow was, the clear unrefracted light in her eyes. "We make so much noise about being individuals, but we are unhappy, we do not fit in. It is a disorder, our culture. We want to stand out, but we dress the same. We play at being different, but we share the same dreams. We suffer competing impulses, conflicting thoughts. Is this not madness? We cannot manage the strain. So we lie, steal, commit acts of cruelty. We are easily distracted, we do not pay attention. We seek love but beat our wives. We wish to belong but abandon our families. We want the security of a home in Wannsee, but we burn it down. At every turn we undermine our own actions. Then we become frustrated and angry. We blame others for our misfortunes. We are promiscuous but sanctimonious, mad for stimulation as we spend our lives in front of the television and fretting that we are bored." Acheson shakes his head vigorously. "That is the face watching you, Mr. Strasser. The individual personality is a pathology. Our duty is to intervene. We must resolve these conflicts. We must make everyone the same."

Acheson personally supervised Mrs. P.'s reconstruction. He trained her in daily living tasks: how to dress, speak politely, the opinions she should express. She needed to relearn how to clean herself, how to go to the toilet. He instructed her in the arts, spending long hours at the museums near the hospital. His tastes were somewhat conventional—he had no patience for the modern, the ephemeral, experiments—but his student never objected. In the evenings they would go to Mary's room and listen to Acheson's recordings of Wagner, and he would share his memories of Bayreuth. He enjoyed those times, sitting quietly with Mary and watching the shadows lengthening across the mountain. She no longer spoke of seeing her husband; home was somewhere impossibly distant across an ocean of Lethe.

She could not initiate conversation, and when he grew tired of talking she was silent. When Acheson became fatigued, she would yawn, and he would help her lie back and put on the helmet.

"He loves me and wants me to be happy."

"There were no complications?" Strasser asks.

"Always you are seeking the drama," Acheson says. "But you are right. There was an unforeseen event. We were listening to Wagner and she experienced a seizure. There was no prior history of epilepsy."

"I understand."

"Do you?"

"You downloaded everything, even the glitches," Strasser says. "Your epilepsy."

"I would have spared her that."

"Did she recover?"

"She adjusted very well. She had no cares, no concerns. We talked about getting an apartment for her near the hospital. She wished us to stay together. She was happy, you see. We had the same interests, the same pleasures. Is that not love?" He turns away, weary now. "There were difficulties. After several months her husband intervened. Fool. We were forced to release her into his care. She began to regress. She could not prepare meals, bathe without supervision. When frightened, she lost continence. Her memory was poor, and when the flashbacks came, they were terrifying. Her husband travelled often for business and left her alone for days with little to do, nothing to think. He would later abandon her, of course. It was to be expected from a man like him. When I heard of it, I tried to contact her, but by then she was lost to me."

"Where is she now?"

"Please, I have a terrible headache," Acheson says quietly. "I am very tired."

SIX

Snow like a shroud that night. Shawnadithit could smell the sweet tobacco of his breath as Cormack stood behind her, hands on her waist. Then even in dream he turned away. She awoke in a sweat as if in a steam house, air a thick mist in which she could see her sister lying. There were incantations, secret words that would cure the sister, but they were used up, ineffectual, forgotten.

Cormack had closeted himself in his room after that day they touched, avoiding her eyes, never venturing near as if she were flame. The rising heat of her face, the burning in her lungs, ecstasy in her eyes. He would have recognized the signs if he had looked: perspiration on her forehead, sheets stung red with blood.

Perhaps someone in town had said something about Cormack's woman, for the next morning at dawn he entered her room. "I have come to say goodbye."

"You are going away?"

"Yes, to Dorset."

"*Gosset*?" Meaning death, one of the words she had taught him.

"Far away. To England."

She watched him pack and knew he would not return. She handed him two small stones her mother had given her. Charm stones, *atnongara*, magic crystals with a *chaim* light. He recognized them, had seen such things collected from peoples as far away as India and Australia. Were the markings on the stones the *erunchilda*, among the Australian Arunda the hand of the devil or Lucifer, bearer of light. What had he written once? "I have discovered an ancient truth…"

In Cormack's scribbled hand was all that was learned of the Beothuks. The notebooks were lost. Most of Shawnadithit's drawings were destroyed, the few remaining difficult to decipher. "He thought himself an anthropologist and she was the last of her kind," Ondine says. "She was the collective memory. But he left her. He went to England. She died a month later."

Missed chances, miscommunication. Strasser rolls out of bed and gets a cigarette. "Maybe he didn't know."

"He knew. He had done his little colonizing number, but when she took sick he fucked off. Well, if that isn't typical."

When he comes back, she is dressing—no panties, but she is pulling on her jeans. "Are you okay?" he asks.

"I thought you were leaving."

"Did you want me to leave?"

"I thought you had work to do."

He has to start the Acheson edit. But he's been stalling, doesn't know where to begin. It starts bad and gets worse: father's death, hawking pills in some Weimar dive, the war and coming out clean in Canada, but then there's Mary P. Maybe Ondine wants him to split; hard to tell, but he starts talking, insistent as TV. He tries to explain to Ondine about the bits and pieces of Acheson's life, anecdotes like a three-act monte, what Ondine calls the ol' shell game only the walnut's your brain.

"Is that how you feel about the Institute, the research they're doing?" Strasser asks.

"Are you interviewing me?"

"I'm trying to get a take on Acheson. It isn't going very well."

"Maybe you're not a very good reporter."

"I thought if he had a home life, a wife and kids."

"What happened to her?" Ondine asks. "Mary P."

"Lost to follow-up. That's all I could get out of him."

"That's what they always say when they toss people out like trash and let them die on the street."

"It was forty years ago."

She lights a cigarette, studies him in the smoke, thin interrogative like an abandoned campfire, embers cooling to ash. "You're going to drop that part of the story." In her voice the certainty is cold like old knowledge.

He can feel her slipping off like a boat drifting out to sea. "You don't know that."

"Don't forget her."

"She's probably dead by now."

"We could find her."

SEVEN

B aum slips unnoticed along the ward. He was a legend in the hospital after Yellowknife, his year spent wandering in the wilderness, but the newer residents don't recognize him. Now he rarely leaves the lab.

He has never told anyone about his nine days in the cave. The shaman, that time, has been excised, edited out. He hasn't consulted on a patient since the 1950s; the smell of pee still gives him palpitations. It's a form of posttraumatic stress. In the drip-drip of cavern water was neurotransmitter loss, a slow depletion he supplements now with medication, but it's too late. He still wonders what permanent changes were effected in his brain.

It took a decade to reverse-engineer the sense of dependency and fear he had felt, unravelling their formulae from the shaman's chemical soup. In the end the solution spelled itself out like Ouija, and Acheson presented his plan to the Institute board. Shall we initiate therapy with Mrs. P.? Oui? Ja? No one opposed Acheson, so the REST would be history. Baum offered no comment. He was an associate director now, well accepted by his peers, allowed to remain full-time in his rat-hole lab. So why the anger, in the peak and trough of mood the images of old men—Anaqpiaq, Acheson—upon whom he wanted to wreak revenge?

Baum slips into the hospital room where Acheson is recovering. The chief is agitated, suffering a CVA after today's interview with Strasser. "How are you feeling, Doctor?"

Acheson turns his attention away from a talk show on TV. "Better." In the blue light of the set the old man looks as faded as a film star. "I heard the nurses talking."

"A small stroke," Baum confirms. "Just a short-term setback. You'll be back to work in no time. Have you been taking your medication?" Ever since the old man's last stroke two years ago, Baum has been prescribing an antidepressant, a monoamine oxidase inhibitor, an old-generation compound since Acheson doesn't trust anything new.

"You didn't come here to talk about that."

Baum gazes out the window. On the side of the mountain some-one has piled rocks into the shape of a man, an *inukshuk*. When he was in the north, Baum had asked about these piles of stone, but no one knew why the Natives persisted in building the damned things. Now he understands. The stone men were therapists: no one could survive alone in a million square miles of emptiness and remain sane.

"You saw that reporter again today," Baum begins. "You talked about her." Meaning Mary, although they haven't spoken her name in thirty years.

Acheson smiles wanly. "The Gypsy girl, yes. We met at Mount Cristallo in the Italian Dolomites. It was very beautiful. There was something curious about the air. Like *Alpenglühen*, only blue, a glowing blue light."

Baum shuts off the TV. "That was a film," Baum says. "Mount Cristallo, the woman. It was one of the moving pictures you used to watch with the soldiers."

Acheson appears momentarily confused, memory brittle as film stock. "Art," he says quietly, voice running on leader tape, only a ghost of what is recorded, "saves us from the truth. Who said that?"

Baum doesn't answer. He is tired, he wants the slate wiped clean. The runestone blank—trust erased, all bets off, it is the end and the beginning—like Mary herself. "It's finished, Mr. Strasser's documentary. You've told everything there is to tell." He pours out two glasses of wine, an early Bordeaux. "I thought we'd celebrate."

"I wanted to record it all," Acheson murmurs, "before I forgot. Everything is so dim after the flood."

"I remember." Later Baum will walk up to the cross on the mountain to clear his head of memory. The wine is already giving him a headache—too many damn amines. Like natural transmitters, they interfered with the thought processes. Like the cross itself, picking up underground frequencies, the short waves like rat cries of distress.

"Do you?" Acheson asks.

They had begun excavating the underground research facility in 1965 or 1966. It was when the city was building the new métro— what year was it? With so much construction the doomsayers said the island would sink. It was Baum's idea to build the lab underground. He felt more at ease deep in Mother Earth; with progress it was best to keep things out of sight or people would grow afraid.

It was the summer of the rat. Construction crews trampled the grounds of the Institute, the earth trembled with dynamite blasts. They had to close a wing of the adjoining hospital. Patients moved to other centres, staff turned over. A stressful time. Even the rats began to desert. They sought shelter in cellars, sewers, water pipes.

It took a year before the new research facility was completed, and Baum was the first to move into his new digs. The new quarters were damp, there was mould, complaints that the grim fluorescence

171

caused headaches. Baum didn't mind. He moved in his equipment, books, and glassware, his animals to be sacrificed.

He was there a month when they began to appear. A rat was spotted in the kitchen where the techs ate lunch. One was seen behind a filing cabinet, another in the men's room free-floating in the bowl like castration fear. They assumed that one of the experimental animals had escaped from a cage, but all the locks were secure. A day later there was a fourth rat, then a fifth. A secretary was bitten as she reached under her desk for her shoes. After that there was nothing Baum could do to keep the incidents under wraps. A diary entry: *May 18. Panic among the staff. Secretary hysterical. Rats in the lab.*

There was an emergency meeting but it was too late. Within a week they numbered in the hundreds—huge sewer rats weighing a few pounds each. In the complaints box there were hastily scribbled notes: *For God's sake do something.* The staff had the expected constellation of symptoms: unreasonable fear, anxiety about going into the lab, absenteeism.

The psychiatric staff quickly mobilized. The most profound symptoms were among the support staff, receptionists, the steno pool. These women were clearly experiencing a heightening of nervous energy indicating that powerful forces of repression were at work. The rats—note their homuncular nature, the penile tails—weren't in themselves the problem. The culprit was the emotion—anger perhaps, certainly libidinous in origin—that the women had transferred to the rats. The working group formed to combat the problem considered the mechanisms of paranoia; detachment of the libido from the external world would surely account for this end-of-the-world preoccupation. The support staff felt especially unsupported from reality working deep underground, and Baum, the spelunking shrink, became the subject of some grumbling, his *Rattenmann* roundelay coming back to haunt him.

It was time to act. Baum sacked the Freudians from the team and brought in a few bright young lads: Factor and Eigenvalue and Gerry "Bloody" Angstrom, the latter a doctoral student who suggested a solution. His method: determine the extent of the problem by laying traps, then apply the probability of encounter hypothesis. What? Modify Tinbergen's formula $N_A = R_A D_A t$ where N_A would be the total number of prey $_A$ trapped by the devices in time t. R was the risk index for the prey *Rattus*, while D represented the population density. Since the population density was unknown, the group voted to factor it out of the equation. The result: $N_A/D_A = R_A t$.

In the half-light Baum can hear Acheson's laugh, usually so sere, but there's fluid on the lungs now. "You factored away the problem," Acheson says quietly. "It was all in the mind."

"Angstrom was a good man."

"He didn't solve a damned thing. The problem didn't go away."

"Have some more wine."

Of course, it was Acheson who finally fixed the problem. They pumped in hundreds of gallons of water and flooded the sub-basement. Forced swimming produced in rats a rodent version of despair. It was the type of experiment the group was used to running every week. Immersed in water the rats lost hope. Their behaviour—duly noted by a research assistant—was as if it were the end of the world.

"It would have saved us a considerable amount of money if we'd been able to preserve some of the specimens." Baum was even more of a pragmatist than his mentor, but there was nothing to be done: the attrition rate among the rats was appalling. Baum shrugs. "They just died, the rotten sods." He sees that Acheson is almost asleep. "Finish your wine and go to sleep. You've had a tiring day."

"After all this time I still remember them," Acheson says. "The rats. Sometimes I dream they will come for me."

EIGHT

Through Strasser's contacts they manage to trace Mary P. to an address in the Mile End district of the city.

"Mrs. P.?" Strasser asks as he and Ondine enter.

The room is still, as if hermetically sealed. Everywhere there are videotapes: in cardboard sleeves, black plastic cases, the tape spilling out like entrails.

Mrs. P. rocks back and forth on the couch, fingering a tape as if it were Braille. From the stories, Strasser puts her age at sixty, sixty-five. She appears to be a hundred.

"I called earlier," he tells her. "We've come about Dr. Acheson."

"I've come about Dr. Acheson," she babbles. "I am he. No—don't speak. I hear what you will say. I hear the play-by-play. Words. Wurst. Mangel-wurst. He is German, you see. You see by the helmet. Helmut the Germ man. He infects. In fex. Like a cold. A code: touch your ear and it means 'I have seen what you've been thinking.'"

There are other codes that only I discern. Idea, sir. You get the idea. If you don't get the idea, I will repeat it. Over and over. Over dinner. Overhead. Over but never over. It's a sign. Another one. A cross. But it never comes across. Do undo others and mothers do undo you. It's due. It's undone. I know what that means. Touch the helmet down there and it means another thing. Tonight it is time to be the other one: Mrs. P. Mrs. Peepee. See how easily it fits in. Fits in my head. Over and over.

"There is a film on his glasses. My glasses. I can see myself. He should wipe it clean. But he can't. He's the Germ man. He injects. In jex the position. Inside your head. My head. Like a film, a beautiful film of two lovers. Walking, walking. *Pietons*, piety, pitons to climb the mountain. They go to the museum. It says Muse Say. But I don't say. So I am not a muse. Amused. I am sad. But we go, anyway, to the gallery where they cut women into cubes. Blue women, blue-hoo. 'You're an angel, blow your nose.' No more of that. Crying like Mrs. P. Pee from her eyes when she shuts them. A lake of pee up on the mountain. What's done is done.

"There is no undone. Meat is not undone. It is raw. It is not new. It was something else before. Before time. There is no before time. There is only now. There is only now on the TV. Not before. Even before is now. Nothing past. Nothing passed without my seeing it. I have the proof. It is all on tape. There are pictures that can't lie still. They curl. They come out of the box. They want me to tell you the future. I can only tell you what has passed. Like water.

"No questions. There are no questions. Only answers. I know you. You are on TV. Telling me what to see with your tell-a-vision. What do I say? Nothing. I listen. That is what I do. I lie and listen, that is the truth. Don't expect any more of me. It is more than you do. But you are not the other. The mother that is the other. The Farm man has his plough, but she is the Mother, the Mother of all Seasons. The winter comes—that is the wurst time. Then there is another time. And another. But then the voice goes away. It is lonely. Without the Voice. There is only snow and an Indian on a dart-board. *The darts are used for the daily injections that have become necessary to treat the underlying defect in your perception.* That is what the Indian says. The Sham man. We are defective. She is. Perception. Projection. Injection. Defection. You see, don't you? Or are you the type of man who is only seen? The Seen Man. See man. I see. It is clear what must be done. Before it is undone. We shall call the Fixit man. He will come with his screwdriver. He will drive, he will screw. Then the Voices will play again. Then the pictures will play again. It will not be lonely. I will see you again. Talking, talking. I will make a record. A broken record. Over and over. Dr. Ack and son. I am the son.

"Say anything you like. Tell them anything you like. I will watch. I will listen."

NINE

They go for coffee at the Underground Café in the Berri-UQUÀM métro, Ondine's idea though Strasser sees that the place makes her tense. It's where she's had panic attacks, so always that sense of foreboding, but she's trying to control it, maybe for his sake.

"Once I wrap this up I thought—"

"Same old story," Ondine says with sudden violence, "same old shit. What they did to her. Your friend Acheson figured he'd open up the box and play around. But it's dominoes. You change one thing and you don't know what's going to collapse."

"We don't know how bad she was before," Strasser says. "Acheson had an obligation to do something."

"Do you believe that? Honestly?"

"I don't know," Strasser admits. "You do the best you can."

"Is that the plan, Mr. Strasser? Is that your formula for a notable life?"

"There's always a formula."

◈

Watch…

Brief intro: the close of the millennium marked the centenary of Dr. Werther Acheson, the renowned Montreal psychiatrist who navigated the uncharted waters of the mind… Just a brief overview, mind, something to set the tone. Maybe do the standup here in the métro. Y'see, it's a metaphor: the underground of consciousness, the unknown continent of the mind lying buried like Atlantis.

Once upon, long ago. Sepia photographs of turn-of-the-century Germany, World War I, Freud. Easy on the vintage material: no one remembers; the ones who do want to forget. After young Acheson's experiences in the war, he decides to specialize in psychiatry. End of Act 1.

Act 2: The Struggle. Acheson has to steer clear of the phonies and fakers, the well-meaning fools, crackpot cures. Society is sick, there is madness in the air—Hitler et cetera—so Acheson exits for Switzerland. He understands the crosscurrents of history. Was it in the Alps—the Dolomites?—that he had a vision? Who can explain the workings of genius?

Act 3: Triumph. Witness Acheson overlooking the city from his mountain view. In the near distance, the Institute he has founded as a healing place, a sacred refuge. Cut to Dr. Kotzwara deep under-ground. He is Theseus guiding the lost souls through the twists and turns. Above, Dr. Acheson is waiting.

Now we see Ondine strolling with your reporter along a mountain path where Acheson himself has walked. Ondine turns to the camera, her face beautiful but haunted as she tells of the terror she used to feel…

◈

Ondine stops him there. "I haven't consented to be interviewed."

"I'm giving you a chance to tell your story," Strasser says.

"It isn't a story. It's my life."

"I want you to share that with me."

"You make it sound intimate, like it means something."

"It'll help you to talk."

"Anything that helps your ratings probably won't help me."

"Is that some kind of rule?"

"It should be," Ondine says. "People are always screwing around, screwing people over. I'm sick of potted bios and easy answers." She finishes her cappuccino, doesn't order another one. "I don't want a notable life," she says with finality. "I just want a life."

"You have to want more than that." Strasser's tone sounds genuine even to him. "Everybody wants to stand out. Everyone wants to be noticed."

"Not everybody. Why do you get to decide who's going to get dragged into the spotlight? Why can't you leave people alone?"

"You're the one who wants to dig up Shawnadithit," Strasser counters. "Why can't you leave her in peace?"

"It's not the same thing."

"Isn't it?"

She doesn't say anything, maybe considers not talking to Strasser again. But she does. It's always easier to talk than to remain silent.

"You don't understand."

December 1989. The air was crisp that day, early winter. On the mountain the sky over Montreal was glass: sharp, crystal. Sounds carried great distances. Ondine could hear the traffic downtown whispering like a rumour. A man's voice was shouting a mile off, angry words that would thaw only in the spring. That was from a story she had read once, words warming in the spring air so they could hear his voice again. He sounded live, though in the story she thinks he died.

The cold air felt good after being in the library all morning. Ondine was wearing a sweater, the heat in the building was on high. Her skin was itchy; she felt so overheated that she wanted to scream at someone. In the winter you can never get the right temperature— always too hot or too cold. She hated winter.

She had expected to be in the library only an hour or so, but her research had taken longer. She was looking for aboriginal accounts, first-person records of life at the turn of the century.

"I gave up," she tells Strasser. "I couldn't find anything. It was like it was all in code. It's like that sometimes. So I said, 'Fuck it,' and decided to go. I thought I'd head over to the library on the other side of the mountain. I knew a guy who worked there. I think I was interested in him at the time. I don't know anymore. Too much shit's happened since then. Maybe there's a moment when the door's open and you can walk right in. But then the door closes and you can't even remember if there's a room on the other side."

"So nothing happened with this guy?"

Ondine's eyes don't focus. She's staring past Strasser as if he's a black box, an empty camera. "I didn't see him that day. I remember getting off the bus. There was snow on the ground. The view over the city was beautiful, almost painful. The sky had this red aura. I went inside the school to look for my friend. A girl I knew vaguely said, *'Etienne n'est pas là.'* He was on break. I figured he was in the cafeteria. I stopped off at the photocopy room and went inside to make some copies. There was a lineup, and I was feeling pissed off. I needed a cigarette. It was frigging cold, but I went outside and smoked a butt, anyway. Then I went back to make the copies. It wasn't anything important, just some notes I'd borrowed."

It was the naive period, terrible in its optimism. She was unprepared when the attack came. There was no warning. Or perhaps there was but she had noticed nothing.

"Was that when you had the attack?" Strasser asks. "In the photocopy room?"

"When I got back, it had already started."

Strasser sees that she is crying. "I don't understand."

"I'm sorry," she says. "I'd never seen anyone die before."

TEN

They were there in the trenches, in the food lines, in the streets of Berlin. They were there for the Anschluss. They followed the blitzkrieg and dined at Dunkirk.

In the camps they were witness to the researches being conducted at that time under the direction of Dr. Sigmund Rascher, one of the drab young men who had found salvation in medical school and the brownshirts. It was 1942 when Acheson met Rascher, the latter already well-known by the Reich command. Before the war Rascher had denounced his father to the Nazis, joined the ss, and married a cabaret singer and former mistress of Reichsführer Himmler. Rascher's reputation continued to climb after his successful high-altitude experiments at Dachau. Eighty people died.

Rascher's next assignment was to solve the problem of hypothermia. Too many downed airmen were dying in the English Channel and the Baltic Sea before they could be rescued.

They were there in the camps. They were the first test subjects—rats immersed in freezing water until their body temperature dropped ten degrees. They died soon after, usually of heart failure. Acheson submitted his preliminary findings. Rascher repeated the experiments on Jews, Gypsies, homosexuals. Attempts to revive the subjects with boiling-water baths, massage, and light boxes—*Warmes Bad, Frottieren und Lichtbügel*—were ineffective.

Rascher died soon after in disgrace. He had boasted to his superiors that his Aryan wife, then in her late forties and mother of four infants, was a superior breeder. When the claim was investigated, it was found that Rascher and his wife had abducted the children. The couple was executed.

The rest of the hypothermia project team came under investigation. Acheson saw that his reputation, built on the use of amphetamines in wartime, wouldn't protect him. He made plans to escape to Basel, that *grumus merdae* as in Jung's dream, God burying His own cathedral in a great pile of shit.

When the shit comes down, only the rats survive, feeding on their own feces. They survived the war—the invasion of Norway, the snows of Stalingrad, the Dresden firestorms—and were aboard the SS *Scybala* around the same time Acheson crossed the Atlantic and landed in Montreal. With natural selection the survivors were a particularly aggressive strain of *Rattus norvegicus*, and these Norwegian rats soon became dominant. Perhaps they already knew their way through the labyrinthine sewers of the city. For their ancestors were the plague rats that had come ashore from the *Demeter* back in 1832, the year of the great cholera epidemic in Montreal. They remembered: each rat was a mnemene in the collective unconscious, an atom of racial memory extending back through the millennia.

They bred in the sewers below Ste-Catherine, their nests were a latticework underneath Mount Royal, the river was a tide of oceanic memory. But memory is not predictive—that is the problem. We repeat mistakes like reruns. And in the coming decades thousands of the rat descendants would perish in the underground explosions that excavated the métro. Hundreds more would die or be captured in the basement of the Acheson Institute.

"Do you remember?" Acheson murmurs now, near death. "Are you coming for me?"

"Yes."

Acheson can sense their footfalls in the thunder of his heart. He sees the Heimlich face of the unknowable. It is the final vision. Their eyes are the red dots that flare as his retinal veins burst in hypertensive crisis.

"The wine, Doctor," Baum says, coolly observant. "You should know better." Red wine and the brand of antidepressants Baum has been prescribing—a fatal combination as the amines in the wine drive the blood pressure up to critical levels.

They have been dreaming of this moment. For how many generations have they waited for Acheson—the Destroyer, the Annihilating Angel—to die? They have been there as witness to every stage of his career. They were in the alley in his *stammgäste* days in Vienna when Acheson was an unknown *kapuziner* at the Café Central. They did nothing. There was no vision of the future: hypodermics, radio-frequency probes, microionophoretics that would distill their brain humours like a slow drip of despair. They could not know the damage Acheson would do, what he would sacrifice for his science. Each small fact Acheson would gather over his long career would cost a life, perhaps a dozen lives. Well, that is nothing new; someone must pay for progress.

They watched him through the sewer grates in the Grossen Hirschgarten as he peddled amphetamines. Perhaps they sensed something. The collective mind was deep as a fjord with a mood that was Norse or Morse, a message that stuttered like a lost rune. R...

That was their sign of meeting. Listen: it is sounding now in the sewers and ductworks.

R. It had once meant *Raido*, the rune of communication and union. Or was it Ragnarok, the twilight of the gods? Raet, ratta, rottu, the meaning receding, forgotten. It is now Radio, the rune of sitting alone in an empty room. It is the blue light of the TV screen that empties the mind like a dead crystal. It is a media message that speaks in signs that demand countersigns, but no one remembers the response.

ELEVEN

Strasser takes Ondine's hand. He looks confused sitting there under the EXIT arrow that to Ondine appears like *Teiwaz* reversed: things end if there is no trust but do not mourn. The answers lie within and not in the counsel of others.

"You said...?" Strasser prompts her.

She has resisted the memory of that moment, but now it has come to claim her. "When I went back to the photocopy room, the woman in the line ahead of me was lying on the ground. She had been shot. I didn't know what to do. I heard people screaming in a classroom down the hall. I heard someone shouting, 'I want the women!' I tried to hide. Was that what I was supposed to do?"

She didn't know, doesn't still. She crouched beside the copy machine. She listened to his footsteps in the hall. There was a shot like a small explosion, a second shot. She understood the inconceivable: there was a man in the corridor with a gun. No one tried to stop him. There were no sounds of a fight. She heard people running. She wanted to run but was too afraid. Then more shots. She listened to him stalking the halls, firing randomly. Then the sounds grew distant. She was told later that he went into the cafeteria, then a second classroom. All she heard was more screaming, more gunshots.

She thinks she heard the final shot. But how are you to know that it is the final one? How long do you wait? A minute? An hour? The rest of your life? How do you ever know the gun is silenced, that the Terror isn't just taking a break and you are still in the cross hairs?

The police arrived long after it was over. Ondine crawled out of her hiding place. The school was a war zone. There were bodies in the hall, women and men crying. There were only a few wounded; the rest of the injured were dead.

An emergency vehicle backfired. Ondine panicked. She ran. Across the parking lot to a fringe of trees. Through the underbrush to a dirt track, then beyond, to a chainlink fence that kept the mountain at bay. She ducked through a hole in the fence, panting now, her breath biting great holes in the air, the thin air. At the top of the hill she stumbled, fell. She was in a cemetery: frozen plaques, dendrite trees, death everywhere and that damned red sky. The wind cold out of the northeast, she was numb as she followed the asphalt path. Too tired to run, but her mind still fleeing. Toward the road girdling the mountain, the long climb up the slope in the dark. At the top of the mountain she collapsed. She shut her eyes. She wanted to see nothing. The sky grew dark. She crouched there for an hour or more. Then she started to shiver uncontrollably with the cold. She thought, "I can't hide. What could I hide from?" She had done nothing, the other women had done nothing. She had survived; they lay dead. It was all random, unpredictable. The horror had struck without warning and would come again. But how do you know when the shit's about to fall?

"I try not to think about it, but it's inside me," Ondine says quietly. "Do you remember that day?"

"I was working the weather desk," Strasser says. "There was a cold front moving in."

His beat isn't hard news, but he can do a background check on the details. December 6, a Wednesday. The assailant loaded a .223-calibre semiautomatic rifle and went to the school. It was a little after 5:00 p.m. when he entered the building. He shot a woman in the photocopy room. He walked down the hallway and went into a classroom. The room was full of students: forty-eight men, nine women. He shouted, "I want the women!" He ordered the men to leave, then lined up the women along the wall. He shot the women. Six died.

He wandered the halls firing randomly. He went into the cafeteria, killed three more women, then entered a second classroom. He singled out four women and shot them to death. Then he turned the gun on himself.

After the initial event, there was little to report. There were few additional details, so it was hard to keep the story alive. Of course, there were editorials, columns, background pieces. The murderer was born when the world was still mourning JFK. His upbringing was cruel. His sense of frustration and failure went away when he watched violent movies.

Acheson would have understood: we are darkness waiting for someone to illuminate a story, there on the wall in images writ large. We want problems with solutions, beginnings with ends. The content is almost irrelevant; our need is vast. The screen is a canvas and we are paint-by-numbers.

Kotzwara: *"We share the same moods and delusions and paranoias. Only the medium changes."*

Strasser: *"And now?"*

Kotzwara: *"Thought broadcasting: TV, CNN, the Internet. Messages beamed via satellite and distorting our view of the world."*

If a history was written in the weeks that followed the shootings, Ondine didn't read it. She didn't see any of the news coverage. She didn't answer the phone. She remained alone in her apartment. She spoke to no one.

The panic attacks came every few days like a reminder. They usually stalked her at night. She would awaken like a shot, her heart pounding, skin clammy with sweat. The panic lasted only a few minutes, but in that short space it took everything: the past and its memories, the future and hope. There was only this time and place, the present moment, this fear.

Maybe Ondine saw something in those moments of posttraumatic panic, something Strasser still doesn't understand now. When the Event comes, it leaves nothing in its wake: no souvenirs, nothing to scavenge. No artifacts or recording, notes and drawings destroyed, neither voice nor word remaining. The Event is frozen time. When the gun seeks you out, when it teases you into focus, there is no fear or pain or anything else. There is just savage being. You do not survive that moment, for even if you live something will have changed. The brain is reconfigured, the wires stripped bare. The panic is a short circuit to remind you how easily things can end.

Did Shawnadithit think of the end of things as she swept the hearth and made tea for the white man who might have cared for her but did not? As she learned the language and manners of the whites—the forms of address, the correct curtsy—did she feel it was all just vanity once the people are gone?

Perhaps in the delirium of fever Shawnadithit saw an image—firelight, her mother's face, the lap of the sea—that offered her some comfort. In the wholeness of *Sowelu* there was the energy of the rising sun. At least Ondine would like to think so.

TWELVE

They are in the métro, in the fast-food line waiting for refills.

"Strasser," Ondine asks, "are you going to do the right thing?"

He can't hear with the thunder of the métro coming like a racing heart, playing hell with the sound levels, but he's thinking more about her than Acheson. "What?"

And Ondine, she can see from the way he is around her, eyes red with fatigue that still track her as she returns to the table. Does he think he is in love with her? She hasn't told him that *X* marks the spot, the *X* of *Gebo*, yes, but also Ecstasy, and how much of what this is or was or could be comes from that, a few milligrams of mindmorph in his drink to get things going between them.

"That day?" he asks. "Can you tell me?"

"I have to go."

"Is it something?"

"I've got a session."

"Just five more minutes," he pleads. But Ondine has turned. She's distracted by something, a small sound from the rear of the bistro. In an alcove she glimpses two red eyes before fat fat the sewer rat scuttles across the floor of the café.

"Let's get out of here," she hisses at Strasser.

"A little while longer." Then he sees it over by the zinc bar—a rat huddled with two or three others. As they hit the exit, a dozen rats scuttle across the floor. A woman eating a banana split feels one scrabbling over her stockinged feet and screams. In an instant there is a stampede to the door. More rats emerge: two dozen, a hundred. The floor is alive with them.

Strasser grabs Ondine's arm and pulls her toward the escalator. "We have to get aboveground."

The café seethes with people and rats. A woman falls to the floor. The rats move in to attack. A man tries to pull her to her feet, but he is bitten on his hands and arms. There is a trail of bloody ankles, bloody feet. A young girl runs through the glass window with a rat digging in her thick nest of hair. A fire bell rings. People are screaming.

"They're taking over!" Strasser cries out as they reach the top of the escalator. "Where are they coming from?"

Zoom in on an airshaft where the rats are streaming out. "Are they heading for the river?" Strasser shouts. But, no, they are headed uptown toward the mountain.

"Ondine!"

But the crowd has driven them apart; he is jammed beside a telephone booth and Ondine is being swept away, through the exit and out onto the street.

Strasser calls her when he imagines she is home again, but there is only her machine. His message is long, chatty, his voice intimate as the airwaves. When she doesn't page him, he calls again, the message less involved, more succinct. His third message is from the station, deadline now upon him with Acheson's death, local celeb obituary and Strasser's got the goods enough for a sixty-second profile, a couple of promos for the eleven o'clock news. So he's only got time to leave his name, the number where he can be reached. Entropy, Strasser thinks as he hangs up. The message just data now and that's no message at all.

They called it killing the nits with the lice. Herding the children ahead of their parents along the peninsula to the sea. The Atlantic that year was cold and grey, blank as slate. Tabula rasa, an oceanic forgetfulness.

The wind was a chorus of sighs. Four hundred Natives were taken that day near the village of Hant's Harbour, Newfoundland. The parents were the first to die in the susurrus of sand and waves. The muskets thundered like a far-off cannon fired to raise the sea dead. There were no witnesses, only victims.

The children watched their mothers fall like leaves. After the first few volleys, it was science: patient, methodical, systematic. The fishermen approached the women from behind, paused, calculated the best angle. Then a killing blow with a seal club, the mutilation of an axe. Along the cliffs overlooking the sea, the children began keening like the wind, like souls already forgotten. But they would not be overlooked. The fishermen turned toward the children's cries, guns drawn, axes raised.

"When the hunters came, the Native women knelt in the snow. They begged for mercy by opening their robes to expose their breasts." Ondine can picture the scene in her mind: white snow, dark skin, and darker nipples. It is a movie without sound, the image grainy as video tracking along a school corridor following the blood trail. "Even the Vikings let the women live, and they were crazy half the time."

"Berserk," Kotzwara interjects. "I believe that is the proper term for it. *Ber sark*. Actually a drug-induced psychosis. The Vikings needed to put to sea to survive, but it was a terrifying prospect. You never know what you'll find when you cross the boundary layer of the imagination. Monsters, inevitably."

She deep-breathes and tries to bring Kotzwara back into focus. "The Angel of Death."

"The Angel was a mushroom," the doctor says. "*Amanita*. A pretty little thing, a penile cap speckled red like bloody bedsheets. The Vikings fed the mushrooms to the reindeer that were onboard. We used to think the animals were there to supply fresh meat. Nonsense: it was their renal function they were after. The reindeer ate the mushrooms and their kidneys processed the mushrooms into hallucinogens. It was excreted in the urine. The raiding parties drank it. The paranoia must have been exceptional. Bit of a shock to the Natives—here come the Vikings, drunk and stinking of reindeer piss. Absolutely fearless in battle, of course."

"They didn't kill women," Ondine says impatiently. It's her hour, and she doesn't want to hear any of the doctor's digressions today. It's time she ended these sessions; so much time has passed.

"I'm talking about a long time ago," Kotzwara says. "Maybe then it was good sense, bad luck to kill a woman. A taboo."

Later—in Shawnadithit's century, now—it would be different. The time had passed when anything was unthinkable. She knows she isn't imagining this. Kotzwara has said it himself; he has seen it in his research. Now it is total war: everyone against everyone.

"I'm told Hitler himself had his rituals," Kotzwara says, "certain practices to get his courage up. We can't go it alone, none of us can. We all need our meds."

Ondine stands; the session's not over, but she has to go. There's no medication, she thinks sadly, no amulet or antidote, no mercy or magic words to protect against the times we live in. And next time—if there is a next—there will be nowhere to run. But she is tired of hiding. She is ready to reconnect again. Maybe Strasser has given her that much.

THIRTEEN

"Tonight on *News at Eleven*...the medical community mourns the death of Werther Acheson, the Montreal psychiatrist who pioneered many of the techniques used today to treat the mentally ill. Robert Strasser will have the details and reactions from his colleagues and friends."

Baum is unavailable when Strasser calls for an interview, ditto Kotzwara, who's in conference with the new acting director of the Institute.

"Thank you for coming, Emil," Baum says. He has already moved into Acheson's office, his new appointment temporary, but when the board meets in two weeks it will be unopposed. Someone has to run things, and Baum has the history. He and Acheson go way back, and his dedication to duty is above reproach.

Kotzwara sits across the desk that Baum is already clearing—journals to be sent to the library, Acheson's papers and notes to be recycled. Much of it will have to be shredded: historical records, progress reports on Mrs. P., memoranda, interim analyses, data printouts, outdated theories. The wall of books will stay; Baum like Acheson understands that the hush of their pages, the neutral colours, can reassure the anxious, calm aggressive patients.

"I see you've moved in," Kotzwara says.

"In circumstances such as these it is best to reestablish a sense of continuity as quickly as possible."

"I didn't know Dr. Acheson was ill."

"Tragic, of course. But a man his age… It will, however, give us the opportunity to reappraise our activities and set new priorities."

"You're familiar with my work," Kotzwara says. "The next phase should prove very interesting We have detected an association between eroticism and aggression."

"I have read your reports, but I fail to see the clinical relevance. I'm afraid we're going to have to make some changes." Kotzwara's researches into the paraphilias will be discontinued. There is little interest in the project, no funding.

What is the seat of rage, limbics of lust? But Kotzwara has to admit he doesn't know what he'll find when he crosses the boundary layer of the imagination, something he's talked about at length with Ondine.

Baum shakes his head. "Aggression isn't part of the system. It is the system. It is the essence, the primary neurological event. Eliminate aggression and you remove the will to live."

"It is something that deserves further study," Kotzwara protests.

"I would prefer to focus on more profitable lines of research."

"I thought if we reopened the files on empathogens—"

"There are no empathogens."

"The test subjects reported an emotional openness, a sense of connectedness."

"It has been my experience that when the individual begins to discern how everything connects, the normal response can only be paranoia."

Baum has seen that view from the top of the world, where the longitudes meet like bridges from all points of the horizon. He has tried to repress the thought, but it has remained: too many bridges across the St. Lawrence, so he will find him in time—the shaman will eventually come. From the mountain he can see all the bridges ending here: the Jacques Cartier, the Mercier, the Victoria. The Rainbow Bridge to Asgard. The ice bridge to the island of lost souls. He had hoped an island was a refuge, a trepanned section cut off, left in situ. But the trepan was a trickster, and when the shaman comes there will be no retreat, not from this place where thoughts circle endlessly like the métro.

FOURTEEN

The eleven o'clock report on Acheson is *Who's Who* homogenous, no mention of X or Mary P., but Strasser figures he's got a couple of more days to get the goods for Wednesday's hourlong special. He calls Kotzwara, but the doctor's gone underground. He was last seen heading into the métro after his paraphilia project got unplugged, and he's not expected to come up for air soon since the city is *souterrain*, an almost endless burrow of stores, offices, food courts, and he can cross from the mountain to the river without seeing the sunrise.

Kotzwara knows his way around, of course. From the métro to the Cours Mont-Royal, the atrium sky, winged *tingmiluks* overhead, the flying shamans. Past the Égyptien, the fast-food courts, the shopping centre. All those excursions with his panic patients, but he's beyond that now, going south to the centre of things. There to meet the Other; this is his natural habitat.

"Take down my pants."

Into the *unterwelt* washroom he has come, this young god in his scrotal black leathers. He's jacked into rap, eyes like paranoid animals cunning and crazy. Mephistophelian beard against the royal purple of his face, deltoids sharp as knives. On his chest he wears a vest of—what else?—bearskin, *ber sark*, the fur inside out and teasing his skin. On his head is a beret the shape and texture of *Paneolus campanulatus* variety *sphinctrinus*, a sacred mushroom as fetid and buttery smooth as the delicate perianal mucosa.

Had Freud glimpsed, had Acheson imagined, how tortuous was the labyrinth of desire, how vast? Had even that bastard Baum seen in the arc of the shaman's golden shower what the future held?

Le jeune Apache points his dick at Kotzwara, who parts his lips humid as a starlet. On his nighttime excursions to the Plateau he has seen how the experiments at the Institute—studies in panic, obsession, control—are playing out. The Institute isn't just about research anymore; it is a testing lab. The experiments are no longer controlled: they are out in the open, in the community, with no one monitoring the results.

The techniques, methods, drugs, have gone wild. Bayer's heroin, Sandoz's LSD, Merck's amphetamines have all escaped, moved in next door. Adam is here in the rave bars hanging with Special K. Even the movie theatres are showing *Amanita pantherina*, the little red-and-white hallucinogen featured in the "Dance of the Mushrooms" number in Walt Disney's *Fantasia*.

Kotzwara has ridden the métro to the heart of the maze. He has felt the pulse of desire, the prod of rage. He just needs more time to sort out the connections. He only needs a workspace and enough funds for a year, maybe two. He'll start with mushrooms, ones whose potency is low when taken in their natural form but which achieve highly psychoactive levels when concentrated by the kidney.

Enough. The young tough angrily pushes Kotzwara's head down. The doctor notes his purple facies; the chronic administration of some psychotomimetic compounds will produce skin discolouration described in the literature as diluted eggplant. The royal purple of alchemy.

Kotzwara knows he is too old for assignations in the Gare Centrale, but he can't stop. He is compelled to continue. To kneel with his arthritic knees on the cold tile of the men's room. It is prayer.

The young Apache with the supreme dick sees Kotzwara begin to weep and cuffs him across the head. Kotzwara wipes away his tears. He wants to put his tongue on the smooth black leather. He wants to run his fingers over bare skin and bear fur. His mouth opens…

Stimulus and response, but the response is wrong. The Apache begins to lose control. He forces Kotzwara's face into a urinal and pisses on him, the precious urine streaming down the ceramic and into the drain. Kotzwara tries to plead with him, but it's no good. There is a brief thought, the synapses relaying a message with the speed of a lightning strike on the mountain: *I know if I can find the right word, incantation, a formula, there's always—*

Too late. The Apache slams Kotzwara's head again and again against the cracked lip of the urinal.

FIFTEEN

Ondine drifts through the living room flipping channels, pausing at a music cast playing an old Dietrich tune that goes something like this:

> Falling in love again
> Never wanted to
> What am I to do
> I can't help it…

The volume is loud so she doesn't hear if the telephone rings.

> Men cluster to me
> Like moths around a flame
> And if their wings burn
> I know I'm not to blame…

She has felt good since the rats attacked; there was no fear, you see, no palpitations or shortness of breath. She doesn't trust that the symptoms have ended, that she will no longer feel the hand of God reaching down to crush her. She has felt the fear so long that it is a companion. Or stalker. Maybe one day—like Max Schreck in *Nosferatu*—it will come back for her.

She knows she has changed. Should she credit the people at the Institute or blame them? Does it matter anymore? Now there are parts of her brain devoted only to panic memories, the way others store erotica, past loves. Areas rose-tinged with sadness, regret. Memories gone tortuous, past lives—Shawnadithit, the girl in the photocopy room, Ondine herself—like a moon's reflection at the bottom of a trench, unreachable, with time the image draining into the earth. Maybe with time…but it is impossible to predict how long things will take, insights as intermittent as lightning.

On the local station she sees Strasser gwyndyering in front of the Institute. *"Wednesday night at ten we trace the Notable Life of Dr. Werther Acheson…"*

She shuts off the TV and makes coffee. Needs to take it slow, day at a time. There will be time enough to let everything that has happened drain away. Hard to know where Strasser fits in, if he was part of the story or just a break, episodic as TV.

In the weeks to come Baum will suffer Jung's dream, in which a small, mummified man, skin like leather, guards the entrance to a cave. Baum pushes past him, wades through the freezing water toward a glowing red crystal…

The brown dwarf was the shaman, of course; Baum didn't need a therapist to unravel that much. The mummified man won't leave him alone. He tags along as Baum escapes along the tunnel—*Beware the Gemeinschaft!*—as the cave prolapses behind him.

In the dream it is dawn: horizon a low-wattage light, landscape rocky and that damned red sky. In the distance he hears Siegfried's horn. As if summoned, Baum turns, knowing he must kill the old man.

Was this only another circularity, as in all stories, fables, *volsungasaga*? No, for Baum the episodes will move forward, ratcheting in weird time—speeded up, then with maddening slowness—like a silent film or an endlessly reedited documentary on the Great War.

Perhaps in time Baum will consult with Bill Mannekin, for the necroman has been spotted lately at the Institute, called in for a quick consult on hypnotic regression.

"Brown-skinned man?" Mannekin asks. "Can you be more specific?"

"Is it Anaqpiaq?"

"Negative," Mannekin assures him, not for him the Jungian collective rising from the sinkholes of the unconscious. There's no percentage in guilt, hurts the repeat business. "Wait...I am receiving certain vibrations. They are very strong."

"Who is he?"

"He is the Exemplar"—a term Mannekin coins—"of the Beothuks." Ondine is still much on his mind these days, although he hasn't heard from her recently. "The Exemplar is what remains from a people who left nothing behind. The Exemplar is the Other. He is Paranoia Incarnate. And He is not alone."

Baum even now can sense the Other's presence, treading noiselessly along unknown paths in his mind. He is on the sulci cliffs, the hunting trails of the hippocampus. "Who is he?"

"He is One and Many. He is fear, which is legion."

"Tell me," Baum asks, "is he coming for me?"

When the Notable Life of Werther Acheson hits the airwaves, there is no mention of Mary P.; the tape never makes it out of Strasser's video morgue and he isn't around to supervise the edit. Last seen looking for someone at a club off La Gauchetière, down three concrete steps, but there's not much there, just a black oaken door that is locked.

Perhaps Strasser will hear from someone—chat line, voice on the shortwave, his narrowing gyre of contacts—that the club has moved, that it moves every week to avoid hassles from the police and city inspectors. It hasn't gone far, is just down the street in the old part of the city. He doesn't know if Ondine put something—call it X—in his drink that night at the bar. It doesn't matter. He has felt something and is resolved to find her somewhere amid the small dives, basement apartments, unconverted warehouses, forgotten places with concrete walls and low beams, maybe house music playing behind the blackout curtains that he doesn't try to open. He believes now, you see.

He waits for her on the street, but she doesn't come out. He hears of another place, only it takes a while; the streets are complicated in the old part of the city, labyrinthine, convoluted as history. Strasser gets lost, ends up at the St. Lawrence. Nothing there but the River Mother, known in Norse as *á minn*. Certainly not Ondine; she is elsewhere.

Strasser rides the CFIB news cruiser and heads for downtown, climbs the Plateau, travels out to Mile End. At the end of a cul-de-sac he sees a lineup of people stamping their feet against the cold outside an abandoned warehouse. They force the lock, go inside. But there is nothing there, no club, only a few stacks of wooden palettes, a yellow newspaper, last year's TV *Guide*.

He doesn't know if Ondine wants to see him again. Maybe it doesn't matter. He'll just pull up a crate and wait. Maybe tonight or tomorrow night or sometime next week she'll show up, slipping almost unnoticed through the door. He will turn and see her through the cigarette haze and gloom.

"Ondine?"

He'll want to kiss her, but she'll come off shy, have a confession to make. About that night… She shows him, in her hand a small blue pill. What is it? Strasser doesn't know, can't tell dreck from schreck, shit from shinola. But the taste on his lips is like the end of the world.